SERIOUSLY?!

SERIOUSLY?!

Stories, Monologues, and Random Stuff

Kate Kasten

Islet Press ✳ Iowa City, Iowa

By the same author

NOVELS
Too Happy
Better Days
The Deconversion of Kit Lamb
Ten Small Beds
Alice's Adventures in Trumpsterland & Alice in the House of Glass
Banners
Lily

SHORT FICTION
Wildwood: Fairy Tales and Fables Re-imagined
Foreign Ground: Stories
*A Little Something for Everyone: Stories, Monologues, Dialogues
    and Observations*
The Mysteries at Sycamore Hill
Cautionary Tales

MEMOIR
Reasonable People: A Memoir
A Certain Time: A Memoir

POETRY
Her Right Mind
Upon Accidentally Knocking an Open Bottle of Olive Oil onto a Wood Floor

Islet Press, Iowa City
kekasten@gmail.com
Copyright © 2025 Kate Kasten
All rights reserved
ISBN: 979-8-9895321-5-5
Book design by Sara T. Sauers
Cover photo by Kate Kasten

CONTENTS

ART

PARLANCE

TRUTH TO POWER

SKIN DEEP

SELF IMPROVEMENT

MODERN LIFE

ECCENTRICITIES

REFLECTION

CONTACT

COME-UPPANCE

PLACE

ART

How to Write Lucrative Fiction: A Guide

HOW DOES ONE "hit the mother lode" and "live high on the hog" with just the use of one's pen (or should I say keyboard)? This simple guide is aimed at aspiring novelists who have been discouraged from their craft by being erroneously told one cannot make a living by writing fiction. I hope fledgling writers will, literally, profit by the advice herein.

RULE 1: LAY IT ON WITH A TROWEL

Let us begin by visiting the work of a best-selling author of thrillers and analyzing his successful method for employing random figures of speech, particularly personification and metaphor. We will limit our discussion to one of his novels in particular, a thriller concerning an inexplicable, awe-inspiring, and ominous symbol that appears in the sky. I have chosen this work because it is especially rich in this author's favored literary devices.

First, let's look at his creative use of personification. If you remember from high school English, personification is the practice of attributing human qualities to abstract concepts or inanimate objects, a practice which the novice writer is often cautioned to use sparingly. However, our best-selling author knows that if you want to stand out from the crowd, you must be willing to break rules.

Here is a sampling from the aforementioned thriller:

"... waving a panicked finger" "The sound of rubber scraping deliriously across asphalt" "He drove by the brooding sedan" "His mind chewed on his plan, once again dissecting every layer of it" "From that cobweb of conflicting thoughts and suspicions, another worrying sound bite rose up. It freed itself, shot up and latched on to her consciousness."

3

A truly bold use of personification.

This brings us to another old chestnut: don't mix your metaphors. Once again, we must compare the income figures of literary novelists who slavishly follow this injunction to that of our maverick author of best-selling thrillers. Would his tale be nearly as thrilling without such complex figures of speech as the following?

> "They crossed the room on tenterhooks and slithered up the stairs" "[He was] made to wield the fruit of his brilliance" "Things were unravelling from all fronts" "His mind rocketed into a manic good news bad news sift-through" "The thought ... was swirling inside them like a tuna-melt well past its sell-by date."

As you can see, this writer courageously pushes his readers' imaginative capacity to its limits and beyond.

RULE 2: CASH IN ON CONFUSION

Next we will see just how unimportant it is to understand the meaning of the words in the metaphors you use as long as you employ them with verve.

What is the purpose of metaphor? Some would say the purpose is to give the reader a vivid mental picture. But is this really what readers want? The writer cited in Rule 1 above might, if we asked him, argue that the reader wants to be challenged by metaphor, made to think. Nowhere in his fiction is this more apparent than in his numerous descriptions of characters' facial expressions. You be the judge of whether these metaphors challenge you—I would go so far as to say defy you—to imagine them.

> "His expression curdled" "His face flicker[ed] with confusion" "His face pinched together with disbelief" "A knot of concentration etched across his face."

We see that, to be effective, metaphors do not need to make sense, in the traditional meaning of "sense."

Before we close the chapter on this author's unique style, I'd like to point out one more significant attribute of his writing which has brought him such a nice chunk of change, or as he might express it, heavy lettuce. And that is his signature use of the verb "nod."

"She nodded stoically" "He nodded enigmatically" "She nodded her confirmation" "[He] nodded warmly" "She nodded ruefully" "[He] nodded his readiness."

One can also admire his generic use of the adjective "tight."

"They exchanged a tight nod" "He acknowledged it with a tight nod of his own" "Then his expression tightened" "Her face tightened at the uncomfortable thought" "His face tighten[ed], drowning with confusion."

We see in these examples the comforting simplicity of repetition, which perhaps serves as a nice counterbalance to the author's otherwise idiosyncratic, often breathtaking figures of speech.

Finally, it's worth mentioning that, unlike many successful authors who illogically express time with the phrase "a long moment," our exemplar employs the more accurate, if self-evident, "a brief moment" as in "…every hair on her body [stood] rigid for a brief moment that felt like an eternity…"

Though his prose is often challenging and enigmatic, it also at intervals provides relief through direct exposition, leaving the reader in no doubt of his meaning, as in "Garbage trucks usually ranked pretty low on the most stolen vehicles lists, which probably had a lot to do with the fact that they were garbage trucks."

RULE 3: RAKE IT IN THROUGH REDUNDANCY

We turn now to one of our most beloved and prolific romance writers and see how she gives the lie to a once time-honored admonition taught in writing academies throughout the literate world; that is, "Show, don't tell." To the contrary, this iconoclastic author's narrative style turns that precept on its head with the approach, "Tell, don't show."

By examining her work closely, we will find that even a reader with mild to moderate dementia, unable to hold a thought for more than one or two sentences, would easily distinguish between the main characters in this author's delightfully ham-fisted *oeuvre*. Let's take a look at a few excerpts from the first twenty-seven pages of a particularly engaging cash cow recently *penned*—if you'll pardon the pun (but, are cows penned or are they pastured? Never mind—not a pun after all)—by this best-selling author.

Her novel features a beautiful, successful film director whose distinctive eccentricity is that she does not care one whit about her physical appearance. The author deftly brings this home in the following, carefully crafted passages:

p. 4: a mass of long, uncombed blond hair piled on her head. ... she braided it into a disheveled pigtail.

p. 9: All she had were the clothes she worked in, which made her look like a homeless person most of the time. [She] didn't care.

p. 10: She had three pencils and a pen stuck in her hair.

p. 11: [She] honestly didn't care how she looked and never thought about it. By looking as though she dressed out of a rag bag, in high-topped Converse sneakers, torn jeans, and T-shirts, she looked like a kid.

p. 13: [She] never wore her newer [Converse sneakers] but only the ones that were torn, stained, and full of holes. Her scruffy look was part of her charm.

p. 15: [She] chuckled as she glanced at herself in the mirror on the visor... "I'm a mess." "Yes, you are," [her assistant said.] "Maybe you should try combing your hair once in a while."

p. 20: [She] looked like a kid ... She still had all the pens and one pencil stuck in her hair.

p. 23: [Eating her husband's excellent cooking] was like going out to dinner ... only better, because she didn't have to get dressed up or even comb her hair.

p. 27: if possible she looked an even bigger mess than she had the day before. She was wearing another pair of ratty, torn denim cut-off shorts with a T shirt that was in shreds. ... "I don't have time to worry about the way I look." She never did. It wasn't on her priority list.

In the first twenty-seven pages, the author adeptly squeezes in 48 separate references to the protagonist's ratty appearance while valiantly attempting a plot. And although I only got as far as those first twenty-seven pages, and cannot say if she continued to keep the reader apprised of how many pencils were lodged in the protagonist's hair, I'm certain I would not have to read the rest of the book to maintain a clear visual image of this nuanced character.

There is, as these examples prove, great money-making potential in prose that piles it on, beats a dead horse, hammers away, goes over the same ground, and gilds the lily.

RULE 4: REPORT DIALOGUE REMUNERATIVELY

Let us return one last time to the bestselling novelist whose prose we examined for Rules 1 and 2. Here we will look at the myriad ways this author avoids using the mundane verb "to say." This writer of thrillers approaches dialogue with an unapologetic distaste for this word. In striving to come up with creative alternatives, he has transformed this simple reporting verb into something daring, sometimes counterintuitive and just a bit startling or simply redundant, as in the following examples:

"I'm not sure," he winced.
"Damn it," he hissed.
"No," she smiled.
"It is," [she] confirmed.
"Sorry," he offered apologetically.
"Okay," she accepted.

On the other hand, a popular police detective series is proof that, it is equally effective to employ that old standby "to say" in every single utterance, as evidenced by the following excerpt:

> "And what makes you think he would know how to find me," Jesse said.
> "If he can work a computer, he could find you," Cronjager said.
> "How?" Jesse said.
> "He could google you," Cronjager said. "I did it myself."
> "Google me," Jesse said.
> "Yep," Cronjager said.
> "Shit," Jesse said.
> "Yeah," Cronjager said.
> "Google," Jesse said. "What does it say?"

It is worth noting that the bestselling author of this series has been dead since 2010, but this in no way deterred the author of this abundantly attributed banter from writing a sequel in 2012. Indeed, why should the series end just because the author has "shuffled off this mortal coil"? Aspiring writers, I can assure you it is quite within the law to keep a beloved series alive by buying the rights to a character. Trust that a significant number of dedicated readers are uninterested in writers' unique "styles" or that the original authors may be resting uneasy in their graves at the liberties taken by their successors. What does it matter who grinds out another sequel as long as one is ground out? The receiver of royalties might as well be you.

RULE 5: SOCK IT AWAY WITH SLOPPY SEMANTICS AND SYNTAX

Another successful strategy of best-selling authors is to shrug off the shackles of semantic precision and bypass with impunity traditional rules of English syntax. Striving for accuracy in the construction of logical sentences can be a time-wasting endeavor if you want to pump those sequels out.

For example, why limit the use of the indefinite article "a" or "an" to indefinite nouns? A few petty self-appointed guardians of grammatical logic object to phrases like, "A smiling Kate" "A radiant Kate," which appear often in a courtroom drama by an author famous for lucrative suspense novels. The indefinite article "a" is for indefinite nouns, these purists cavil—*a box, a thought, a love affair*—<u>*not*</u> *a smiling Kate, as if she were one of several smiling Kates!* But sheep-like adherence to grammar rules will not put an author on easy street. Do not hesitate to bring "an incredulous Brian," "a bemused Amanda," "a startled Fletcher," or "a dyspeptic Rick" into the room.

Another writer, the author of at least 20 suspense novels, has learned to tidily bundle contradictory actions into one sentence, thereby economizing on word count and sidestepping the need for the unimaginative conjunction "and." Try it with these quotes:

> "Crossing the living room, [he] searched the hallway." "Entering, the two men stood." "Standing, he walked back to his house."

Why separate the actions just because they are incompatible? This author rightfully expects his readers to do the work for him, to make that jump of logic by proactively supplying the sequence in their heads. "Kissing him," he writes, "[she] walked off to take a shower." Do you need to be told that she kisses him first and *then* walks to her shower? If the reader does believe she is kissing him and walking at the same time, I say more power to the image.

Similarly, a prolific author of historical fiction has found that attributing feelings to inanimate nouns can save the 3-5 extra words needed to link the emotion to an actual person. Referring to a "shocked aftermath," "discomfited red dye," "embarrassed haste," "a skeptical challenge," "grateful surprise," "bewildered pain" "apologetic ignorance," and so forth, kept her 931-page novel from hitting that daunting thousand-page mark. Something had to be sacrificed. Logic? Or scenes of medieval fornication, of which the author had already shown regrettable restraint by limiting herself to only fifty-one.

RULE 6: GETTING GOBS OF THE GREEN STUFF WITH GROTESQUERIE

Finally, we will answer the frequently asked question, "How do I hop on board the ghoul gravy train?

To begin with, it is worthwhile to point out that getting ahead with the undead is a time-honored tradition, beginning with Mary Shelley's 1818 sensation, *Frankenstein* and Bram Stoker's 1897 shocker, *Dracula*.

So how about you? How can you be in clover by raising your protagonists from under the clover? Two words: zombies and vampires. Take any already extant narrative—from a Jane Austen novel to a modern day bodice ripper—and turn the protagonist and one or two additional main characters into walking corpses.

Is it really that simple? Yes. It is. The story line is already written for you. All that's required is to change the heroine's complexion from that of a rose in full bloom to that of a lily atop a coffin. The rest will flow naturally. Or, *super*naturally, as it were.

Before ending this section, I would like to add an aside, somewhat off the topic but not entirely unrelated. A word of caution to those of you writing in the genres of the murder mystery or the thriller. If you seek to procure your bonanza with butchery, do not censor yourself upon considerations of basic humanity or the misguided impulse to be original. You cannot go wrong if you stick with this fail-proof formula: abduction, torture, rape and murder of women and/or children. Don't disappoint your readers with anything less.

CONCLUSION

It is my sincere hope that if you believed your inspiration had perished forever, this modest guide has revived it; furthermore, that you now grasp why writing lucrative fiction is within anyone's reach, and that you can find the courage to write that novel you have long nurtured in your bosom, no matter how hackneyed you know the prose to be.

Against all probability, many writers have achieved "success by the sack full" through their literary endeavors. There is nothing to stop you from joining the ranks of that happy band.

Shakespeare Run Amok

IT'S SATURDAY AFTERNOON. I'm washing up the breakfast and lunch dishes when I suddenly come to an abrupt halt. Oh my god, is this the day we're performing those Shakespeare scenes at my house?

I haven't even begun to learn my lines. I hastily open my calendar. Oh, thank goodness. It's *next* Saturday. Relief! Still, I'd better start memorizing, ASAP.

At that moment, the doorbell rings. There at the doorstep are the cast and crew, along with Sebastian, the director, who takes himself very seriously.

Oh no. It *is* today! I wrote down the wrong week!

This is just an amateur living room production for donors and supporters of the theatre company, but Mr. Director pushes his way in and is soon bustling around officiously as if he's at The Globe. He's giving orders: where to hang the sheets for the back drop and precisely where to position the makeshift props. Folding chairs for the audience are being brought in and set to face the improvised stage at the end of my long living room.

How can I tell him? I must be brave.

"Sebastian, I'm afraid I have bad news."

"Not now, Judy. I need to concentrate." To a teenager, pinning a home-made banner with a magic-markered coat-of-arms on the sheet, he yells, "NO! Not *there*, Jeremy, for god's sake! To the *right*! To the *right*!"

I wonder what Sebastian's parents were like. It's probably not by chance that they gave him a handle that doesn't lend itself to nicknames. It sounds like the kind of name that precedes a scolding. "Se*bas*tian! Get your feet off the coffee table!" "Se*bas*tian! Don't say 'Gee'!" "Sebastian, no dessert if you don't eat your spinach!" And what indignities did the man suffer as a child when classmates on the playground called out, "Seba-a-astian" "Seba-a-astard."

I hate adding to his trauma, but I must. "Sebastian, I thought the performance was *next* week. I don't know my lines. I'm sorry."

He stops and gazes at me coldly before turning away. "Well, do your best. If you flub a line, just keep going."

"No. I mean I haven't *begun* to learn my lines. I don't know them at all. I haven't actually had time to read the scene yet. I'm not really sure what happens in it. I mean, I *sort of* know. I think I studied it in high school. Or *some* Shakespeare anyway."

He turns back to stare at me in disbelief. "It's the *balcony* scene. Romeo and Juliet. Don't tell me you haven't read it, and you don't know what *happens*? Have you been living under a *rock*?"

I resent the implication that I'm a maggot.

It's *Sebastian's* damn fault anyway for thinking we could do this performance without rehearsing.

"I've never done Shakespeare before. I'm more of an Edward Albee person."

He sits down on one of the rented chairs and shakes his head in a stunned manner like he's just received the telegram with the news that he's now a Gold Star parent.

"You've still got the other two pieces to showcase, Sebastian. I'm sure Mike and Tyler and Ginnie and Mason will do a great job. I mean, I know it'll shorten the performance, but—"

"It's *already* too short as it is."

And whose decision was that?

He stares at the stage disconsolately.

Then inspiration hits me.

"Sebastian! Hold on! I have an idea."

He looks up with jaundiced eye. "I can't wait to hear it."

"No, really, it'll make the scene even better than if I'd learned the lines."

I take the seat next to him, which abruptly drops a couple of inches because it hadn't been completely opened out. "Yikes!" I exclaim. Sebastian scoots his chair away as if my chair's aberrant deportment might be contagious.

"So here's my idea. Gerald will speak *his* lines, and I'll just make *up* mine. Won't that be *droll*? See? There's a Shakespearean word. I think."

He narrows his eyes. A skeptical eyebrow is raised. "You think *you* could pull that off?"

No, not at all.

"Sure!" I say. "It'll be a little wacky."

"Whatever." (An expression I couldn't have imagined escaping his middle-aged lips.) "I wash my hands of it." He gets up and stomps off toward the "stage" to bark at another volunteer.

The audience is already beginning to drift in. My scene is first. No time to even glance at the script, which is just as well since I couldn't find it the other day when I went looking for it.

The dimmer switch brings down the living room lights. I clamber into position, precariously balancing on a kitchen chair. Gerald is on one knee looking upward.

Sebastian stalks onto the stage and slaps his hands together in lieu of a clapboard.

SEBASTIAN
Romeo and Juliet, Act Two, Scene Two

[High-powered flashlights clamped to step ladders come on to illuminate the "stage."]

ROMEO
"But, soft! what light through yonder window breaks?
It is the east, and Juliet is the sun.
Arise, fair sun, and kill the envious moon,

Who is already sick and pale with grief,
That thou her maid art far more fair than she:
Be not her maid, since she is envious;
Her vestal livery is but sick and green
And none but fools do wear it; cast it off."

[For the next line Gerald exaggerates his double-take:]

[Staggering.]
"It is my lady, O, it is my love!
O, that she knew she were."

[Etc. … blah blah blah blah blah …]

O, that I were a glove upon that hand,
That I might touch that cheek!

[There's a pause while I start to realize he's finished.]

JULIET
O *Do* it! I dare thee!

[Audience emits an audible gasp.]

ROMEO
[Gerald is literally speechless, looks offstage for a moment as if hoping
for a prompt. Finding none, he declaims …]

"She … speaks:
O, speak again, bright angel! for thou art
As glorious to this night, being o'er my head
As is a winged messenger of heaven …"

[And so on …]

"… And sails upon the bosom of the air."

[He closes his mouth decidedly. Apparently it's my turn. I hesitate. His back to the audience, he mouths O *Romeo, Romeo*. I do recall hearing this line before.]

JULIET
O Romeo, Romeo, dost thou speaketh of my bosom?

[The audience titters. I feel encouraged.]

ROMEO
[Aside] Shall I hear more, or shall I speak at this?

[He waits, seeming to want the actual answer. I oblige.]

JULIET
We were speaking, were we not,
Of bosoms?

[Gerald looks appalled. He casts a glance toward the wings, hoping, I suppose, for a prompt. Sebastian is standing against the wall, clutching his script in a troubled manner. No prompt is forthcoming, so I must move the plot along. A line comes to me (from whence, I do not know). Whatever. I say it.]

JULIET
A rose by any other name would smell as sweet.

[I get the impression this line is premature, or perhaps not mine. Gerald, against his better nature, is forced to improvise.]

ROMEO
Nay, but tarry awhile, unless you fear the wrath of *Capulet*.
Thy *namesake*. Just as I am *Montague*.

[I gather the subject of names is à propos here. I'm Capulet. He's Montague.]

JULIET
Good names and pleasing to the ear.
Especially Capul*et*, to go with Juli*et*,
Having assonance, rhyme,
And alliteration to boot.

[One punctilious-looking gentleman in the first row appears to have a *Collected Works* on his lap and is, seemingly, searching the pages for that speech.]

ROMEO
[Baffled, but recovering.]
I know not how to tell thee who I am.
My name, dear saint, is hateful to myself
Because it is an enemy to thee.
Had I it written, I would tear the word.

JULIET
[An aside.] Methinks the fellow doth protest too much.

ROMEO
[Grasping at straws] O wilt thou leave me so unsatisfied?

JULIET
'Tis thine own fault
with stimulating talk of bosoms.

ROMEO
[Perhaps to change the subject (his brow having broken out in beads of sweat):]

O blessed, blessed night! I am afeard.
Being in night, all this is but a dream,
Too flattering-sweet to be substantial.

[Ah, I sense that that's my cue. We're back on track.]

JULIET
To sleep, perhaps to dream.
To dream of hands that ne'er will be clean.

[Gerald looks agonized. The floor is uncarpeted. He shifts to his other knee.]

ROMEO
It is my soul that calls upon my name.

[I hadn't called his name but do so now.]

JULIET
O Romeo!

ROMEO
[Looking relieved.]

How silver-sweet sound lovers' tongues by night,
Like softest music to attending ears.

JULIET
What? Tongues as well?
My lady mother'd not approve.

ROMEO
[He adlibs. Gives it his best shot.]

Therefore thy kinsmen—uh …
Kins*woman* … is no stop to me.

[Then back, I surmise, to somewhere in the script.]

With love's light wings did I o'erperch these walls,
For stony limits cannot hold love out,
And what love can do, that dares love attempt.

JULIET
Even so,
Good night, good night, Sweet Prince!
Parting is such sweet sorrow,
that I shall say goodnight
'til it be morrow.

[Gerald frowns fiercely. But I'm on a roll.]

Such earnest sentiment.
Like unto poetry,
I canst but repeat.

Good night, good night.
Parting is such sweet sorrow
that I shall say goodnight
'til it be morrow.

[Then, perhaps I overdo it a touch.]

A thousand times goodnight.
Good night Good night Good night
Good night Good night Good night.
Tomorrow and tomorrow and tomorrow
Creep along day in, day out.
And all our days are yesterdays.
[I sigh] Ay me.

Gerald's mouth's agape so that he is like unto a fish.

[Oops. Did I say that aloud? Some in the audience look shocked. The rest cover their mouths to hide *their* mirth.]

ROMEO
[Interrupting feebly, his voice cracking.]

A thousand times the worse to want thy light.

[Perhaps I should have acquainted Gerald ahead of time with the plan. He frowns and squints, as if searching his mind for a speech from an earlier page. Seems relieved to find his exit line.]

ROMEO
Sleep dwell upon thine eyes, peace in thy breast!
Would I were sleep and peace, so sweet to rest!
Hence will I to my ghostly friar's cell,
His help to crave and my dear hap to tell.

[ROMEO limps off, RIGHT.]

JULIET
[Having the last word, I call after him.]

Through all thy hints of breasts,
Of bosoms and of tongues,
Wilt thou leave *me* so unsatisfied?
'Tis a changeable gentleman
Forsakes a lady upon
Occasioning her rut.
Is "rut" the *proper* noun?
Perhaps not proper, but …
What's in a word?

Never mind.
I'm out of here.

[EXIT JULIET LEFT.]

[The audience rises as one, with thunderous applause and a demand, "Encore! Encore!"]

> JUDY [offstage, sotto voce]
> The performance was a triumph,
> though I do say it myself.

CURTAIN

I didn't begrudge Sebastian elbowing me out of the way to take center stage for the bow. I was gratified to see the brightness of his cheek and his eyes twinkling in their spheres.

Slime: an Ode
(A performance piece)

I'M JUST RECOVERING FROM a raging head cold. I've been snuffling and snorting and clearing my throat and hacking and hockering and blowing my nose for a week. I blow my nose for a whole minute. My brains are starting to come out. And then a minute later I have to do it again. ... How does a body produce all that? Where does it come from? It's kind of ... awesome.

It inspired me to write a poem. It's pretty good. I think you'll like it.

> Slime is everywhere ...
> Slime laps the shores
>   of green lagoons,
> Slime haunts the drawers
>   of Frigidaires.
> Leaves its mark
>   on underpants ...
> Reminds us of the lunch we
>   tried ...
>   but could not digest.
>
> Slime asks no questions ...
>   knows no answers.
> Slime seeps out of every orifice ...
> It coats our brains, our
>   stomachs ...
>   and our hearts.
> We cannot think, cannot
>   sense or feel ...
>   without slime.

When the world
        has all but come apart,
Slime is the glue.

Slime knows no boundaries,
Respects no limitations.
You cannot pick up slime
        ... or put it down.

Slime is timeless.
When the earth on its axis
        halts ...
Still remaining ...
Still enduring ...
Two elements:
        Time ... and ... slime.

Thank you.

Talking Books

I LISTEN ADDICTIVELY to audio books. Good books, bad books, that's irrelevant as long as the plot keeps me streaming.

However, I'm not so tolerant when it comes to the readers of these books. If you've listened to audio books, you know that a good reader can make even a pathetically written story sound brilliant. And a bad reader can make a brilliant story sound inane.

For example, take a recently published best-seller about Abraham Lincoln written by a highly respected historian. The author's prose is clear and crisp. The information is meticulously researched. The characterizations are vivid and fascinating. The story is easy to follow. It was just what I needed to distract myself from my obsessive thoughts about the current political fiasco.

The story starts with this sentence: "On May 18th, 1860, the day when the Republican Party would nominate its candidate for President, Abraham Lincoln was up early."

But here is how the first sentence was actually read: "On May 18th, eighteen six-tee, the day when the Republican Pah-ty would nominate its candidate foh President, Abraham Lincoln was up uhly."

This is the so-called Mid-Atlantic accent. I would like to take this reader out to the Mid-Atlantic and throw her in. But. I tell myself, don't be judgmental. Other people—not me—but other people—might find this voice pleasant and cultured. Although these would be people who, themselves, speak as if they were auditioning for the role of Mrs. Teasdale in Duck Soup. (Affected British accent. A Marx Brothers reference. Never mind.)

This book is seven hundred fifty-four pages, which translates to forty-two hours of listening to the Mid-Atlantic accent. The reader goes on in this vein: "When ahsked in 1860 [six-tee] by his campaign managuh [manager], John Locke Scripps, to sheh [share] the details of his uhly days, he hesi-ta-ted. 'Why Scripps, it 'tis a great price of folly to attempt to make anything out of uhly life. It can ohl [all] be condensed into a single sen-tence you will find in Gray's Elegy. 'The showt [short] and simple annals of the poah [poor].'"

She's quoting Abe Friggin' Lincoln! The man learned to read by candlelight. He made a living by splitting logs. Why does she make him sound like James Lipton from Inside the Actors' Studio? I'm listening to this book, walking around my house, tearing my hair, screaming "TALK REGULAR!"

But, it's my own fault. I should just get the print version and read it to myself out loud.

There's another problem with audio books. Many of them aren't available for streaming, so you have to listen to them on CD. I find, as I prepare for bed, that if I put the CD player next to my pillow and insert the book—something utterly lacking in suspense, like an Agatha Christie novel, read by an actual British reader in a contemplative, soothing voice—I slip into a peaceful, worry-free sleep before the reader gets to track two. And then I have to start with track two on the following night, taking me three months to get through the whole book, albeit with a somewhat spotty understanding of the plot.

However, that is all theoretical. In fact, what happens is this ... I'm just drifting off to the words "Ah yes, Miss Marple. It's quite an old tree. It's called a black elm. BlaKelum Blakelum kelum kelum kelum kelum." Someone has scratched the CD and returned it without owning up. I start awake, heart pounding, expecting Jack Nicholson to crash through the bedroom door with an axe.

This is the downside of books on CD. The only remedy is to call your local library every day and find out which books on CD arrived from the publisher that morning, then run down to the library and check them out while they're still in mint condition.

Apart from that, you'd better just do it the old-fashioned way. Read the damn thing.

Too Much Heaven

IT'S CALLED "CLICKBAIT." Isn't that a great word?

I was looking for a Kitten-Sleeping-On-A-Golden-Retriever video that I hadn't already seen, when YouTube's logarithm threw up the suggested video options along the right side of the screen.

Wait. Logarithm? Is that the word? Or … *Algorithm*. That's it! They spy on you all the time. But I won't go into that here.

Anyway, this video popped up, probably because YouTube knew I was interested in World War II. It's the Andrews Sisters in uniform singing "Boogie Woogie Bugle Boy" to a bunch of GIs. Before my time, I know (I was born in 1946) but pretty good stuff—that close harmony, that swing, that pizzaz!

I wasn't looking at just the sisters singing, though. It was a split screen—is that the term? The sisters on a small screen in the lower left corner, superimposed on a larger screen with two people—reactors—watching the act. The reactors are kids. Well, to me they're kids. In their twenties or thirties, I'd guess. They're going nuts over the Andrews Sisters. With no idea what era they came from.

"This is real old school," the girl says. "Like 1980s? Or maybe 1960s?" (Ha!)

The boy says, "What's a bugle?"

But they're grooving to the sound and—as I say—to the pizzaz.

Well that was the start for me. I'd never heard of this thing called Reaction Videos or First Time Hearing. It consists of one, or often two, of these twenty- or thirty-somethings listening to the music of my generation and earlier. I couldn't get enough of these videos. And *especially* when the algorithm put me onto reactions to Bee Gees' "Too Much Heaven."

I need to be forgiven for not paying attention to the Bee Gees back in the day. I had a boyfriend who loved them, but pop music didn't interest me. I kind of disdained it. In fact I wasn't really a music person at all at the time. *Still* not. Until *now*.

So, suddenly these reactors appear, listening to "Too Much Heaven" for the first time in their lives—

Wait, let me go back. Apparently these reaction videos are a major fad, starting in 2007 (I found this out later—thank you, Google). And from what I've seen, the reactors are generally young people who love music, and many who are musicians themselves. But they'd never been exposed to the music of their parents and grandparents. ("Old school.") So now they're making up for lost time. You can't imagine what a kick it is to see these kids getting their minds blown.

I watch it on my desktop computer. Take, for example, this video of Bee Gees singing "Too Much Heaven." First of all, the production values of the video are outstanding. The Bee Gees are performing in what I think is a large studio. They're surrounded by an orchestra—violins, horns, guitars, drums, the works—and the orchestration is superlative. To say nothing of the camera work. It pans slowly around the room and lands on the three brothers dramatically lit by a single spotlight.

By the way, are you *aware* that the Bee Gees were brothers? (Again, thank you Google.) Born in the UK, raised in Australia, returned to the UK to advance their career. They'd been singing together since they were little boys. The whole family was musical—five kids, mom and dad—all singers and instrumentalists. Plus, the brothers wrote all their own songs: "Stayin' Alive," "How Deep Is Your Love," "Night Fever," etc., etc., etc., as well as songs for others. Over a thousand compositions.

Anyway, picture these guys. Shirts unbuttoned to the waist, skin-tight pants, thick wavy hair I would die for. On first sight they're a seventies stereotype, and then they *open their mouths.* Too ... Much ... Heaven.

Here's where my attention shifts to the reactors. You watch their *first* double-take—the furrowed brow, the head tilt—then the second double-take—the silence, the dropped jaw, the goggling eyes. After that, the grimace, as if they've just taken a blow to the gut. Their eyes are squeezed tight, faces all scrunched up, heads shaking: "No, no, no, no, no, no!" "This can't be happening!" "This isn't possible!" "How? How? How?" "It's *fire!*" Then the smile, ear to ear, a burst of joyous laughter. Arms flung in the air. Expletives and obscenities: "Oh shit! Jesus Christ! What the f—?" One reactor leaps onto his swivel chair and crouches there, hugging his knees, so blown away he doesn't know what else to do with himself.

Finally comes the trance-like head and shoulder sway, the dreamy smile. (But why aren't they *weeping? I'm* weeping.)

And it *is* happening, *is* possible. Right before their eyes and ears. The Bee Gees. Real voices in real time, coming from actual mouths and lungs. Quiet power. No digital mixing, no layering.

Some reactors, after listening to a few bars, say, "This's gotta be Auto-Tune!" I'd never heard of Auto-Tune, but I could guess the general idea. Because every breath, every pause, every note is perfectly in sync. All the harmonies and the vibrato blend as a single voice. I wikipedia'ed Auto-Tune. Hello-o! Guess what, you skeptics. Auto-Tune didn't exist until 1996. "Too Much Heaven" was recorded in 1978.

All three Bee Gees leaning into one microphone. The smooth *falsettos!* And don't get me started on these guys' faces. "Angelic" is the cliché that all the reactors ultimately resort to because otherwise they're "speechless," they "have no words," only "Wha—?!"

"Nowadays," a reactor grumbles, "all the big time singers gotta have their retakes—'Help get me in B flat!'"

Another reactor complains, "Our generation is horrible. Dude! What we have is crap."

Despite this self-criticism, these young reactors are so *happy!* That's what pulled me in. How often do you get to watch such profound appreciation, such pure joy, unadulterated bliss, exuberance? It's contagious. I can't get enough of it.

It turns out you can type in the name of practically any singers from the past and find contemporary reactions to them: The Righteous

Brothers, The Supremes, Aretha, Carole King, Johnny Mathis, Linda Ronstadt, Dolly, Ella Fitzgerald. Even Tom *Jones*, for cryin' out loud!

But I have to admit I'm stuck on the Bee Gees' "Too Much Heaven." I'll bet I've watched various reactions to that clip thirty or forty times this week. I know I sound obsessed. But it's a good kind of obsession. It keeps me away from the political horrors unfolding as we speak (twenty-two days to the 2024 election—help!).

I'm watching every reaction I can find (there are an infinite number) to "Too Much Heaven" and I'm choked up, tears streaming down my cheeks. The euphoria!

I sit for hours at my monitor (did I mention I don't have a cell phone?).

...

My granddaughter Carla: Grandma! You don't have a *phone*?! That's crazy!

Me: I do have a phone. I have a landline. Why do I need a cell phone? (She's appalled.)

Anyway, I'm reacting to these reactions. Fascinated. And I wonder at myself. Such emotion I'm feeling! Who is this ecstatic old woman practically glued to the screen. *Just one more video* and I'll go to bed.

And I'm thinking, I should join those reactors on that split screen. React to their reactions. Make it a *two-tier* reaction! So meta!

How would I do that?

Carla: "Yeah, I could set it up, Grandma. You have a webcam recorder, don't you."

Me: Do I?

Carla: Right there on top of your computer from when I fixed you up for the Zoom call.

Me: Oh. That's what that is? I'd forgotten.

Carla: Or you could use Tik Tok or Instagram on your pho—. Oh, but you *don't have a phone* (she frowns at me severely). But do you care about the quality?

Me: Sure. I want it to look good. And sound good, especially the "Too Much Heaven" clip.

Carla: OBS would give you the best quality.

Me: OBS?

Carla: Recording software.

It's too much for me to grasp. She volunteers to take care of the whole thing. (See, this is why everyone my age needs grandchildren. Even my great grandchildren could probably handle this, and they're still in elementary school.)

...

So Carla's finished setting me up. I have a *channel* now (or whatever it's called). You can watch it if you type in GrandmaReactsx2. Not very original, I know, and kind of condescending, like, Oh, look at this! A *grandma* reacts? A *little old lady on YouTube*? But I'm not the creative type. I couldn't think of an imaginative identifier.

For the filming, I wore a tasteful but modest cardigan with a stand-up collar (no reason to call attention to my turkey neck) and sat on a stool (*not* a rocker, thank you very much), finger hovering over the pause button.

Anyway, there I am, filling most of the screen. The two smaller images—clips of the Bee Gees singing and reactors reacting—are overlaid at the bottom. The sound quality is excellent.

GrandmaReactsx2's reactions to the reactors' reactions tend to be more subdued than theirs but do seem to follow a sequence. I notice that *my* first double-take, like theirs, is the furrowed brow and a head tilt. But from there, I go right into the ear-to-ear grin.

Then the second double-take—instead of the head shaking and *no no no no no*, it's head nodding and *yes yes yes yes yes*. No grimace (I wouldn't want to put my lip wrinkles on display), but definitely the burst of laughter and hands flung up like the hands of Christians at a revival meeting.

My expletives and obscenities?—"Oh man!" "Whoa!" "Yikes!"

"Damn!"—and I have no problem letting jubilant tears spill over and fall onto the console.

"Too Much Heaven." Is it really such a good song, you ask? Watch GrandmaReactsx2 and judge for yourself.

> *Nobody gets too much heaven no more.*
> *It's harder to come by*
> *I'm waiting in line.*
> *Nobody gets too much love anymore*
> *It's as high as a mountain*
> *And harder to climb.*

And that's just the first verse.
Yeah.

To Get the Juices Flowing

OKAY, SO YOU'RE STUCK FOR inspiration, a new idea, a topic, a plot, a theme, a tale, a first sentence. Something to get you going. Here's an old standby taught universally in writers' workshops:

With your eyes closed, open a dictionary and let your finger land on a random word or phrase. Write it down. If you don't know its meaning, write the dictionary definition next to it or just guess or go with what it makes you think of. Carry out this procedure three times so you have a list of three words or phrases.

Start to write, incorporating either the words themselves or their meanings or associations. The thing is not to think about it or plan or try to organize your thoughts. Just let the pen (or keyboard) do its work and see what it comes up with. Try not to censor anything that comes to mind. (And so as not to be tempted to censor icky, embarrassing images, don't anticipate reading it to anybody. It's strictly free association for its own sake.)

Stop when you've had enough. You don't have to complete what you've written or come to any conclusion or revise. You may or may not have produced something you will want to develop later.

Got it?

So here's what came wandering out of my brain the last time I undertook this procedure:

Words: *Mediterranean*
       Staging
       Jump

The **staging** area was to be **Gibraltar**. A thousand gay fluttering sailboats would be lined up below the monolith like a lei necklace and at the single report of a thousand champagne corks going off simultaneously they would set out across the **Mediterranean** for the shores of Morocco. It was a mad race made madder by the presence of so much champagne and so many people in bright evening dress **jumping** overboard and having to be retrieved by rival vessels.

Words: *Wagon*
       Dilator
       Apalachee Bay (inlet of the Gulf of Mexico
         in northwest Florida)

The Apalachee Indians used a special herb found only on a single inlet of the shores of the **Apalachee Bay**. They used it to **dilate** the eyes of their enemies. It was a kind of primitive chemical warfare used successfully for centuries on their traditional tribal adversaries. It was a deeply-held secret known only to the old medicine women who made the concoction, and the warriors who sneaked into their enemies' tents at night and sprinkled it on the embers of their fires. In the morning the affected braves would stumble around in a blinding world from which they would only emerge in the other side of life because, unable to see, they would be easily killed off by the cunning Apalachee warriors who walked confidently into their camps armed only with a tomahawk.

Those were in the days before all the tribes gathered in a spirit of cooperation to thwart the invasion of the white people, who had converged on the region in boats by sea, and **wagons** by land. The presence of white intruders drew the tribes together at last. They put down their weapons, and their medicine women convened in the women's lodge and the warriors in the men's to discuss the efficacy of using the blinding herb on the whites. The problem was that these white-colored people did not sleep in easily accessible tents with fires smoldering inside. They slept in their boats or in the beds of their wagons with their fires smoldering in the open air which grabbed the smoke and took it to the heavens where it could do no harm. The herb had to be applied in a different way.

Words: *Spiniferous*
       Clara
       Vaseline

Margery was hiding in the attic behind a set of shelves that held mammalian and crustacean specimens. She peered out over a **spiniferous** stuffed creature—headless now and so covered in dust you couldn't tell if it had once been a needle-wielding porcupine or a sea urchin.

Clara Schumann's face beamed encouragingly down at her from the wall under the eaves where it was encased in a huge gilt roccoco frame that dwarfed the smiling ignored sister of the adulated composer.

Margery was smooching and squooshing her face about in an effort to pop off the plaster-gauze life-mask before her sister could come up and find her. She had refused to put **Vaseline** on under the gauze because she hated feeling oily. She wouldn't even eat chicken because of the sensation on her lips and fingers and chin. Her sister had insisted the mask would stick to her face when it finished drying and she would never get it off if she didn't smear her cheeks with Vaseline first, but Margery had been adamantly opposed to the idea and now she was crouched down behind the curio cabinet in a panic over the mask—not because she was especially worried about having to wear it for the rest of her life, but because she would rather go into permanent hiding than suffer her sister's condescension.

Words: *Selectman*

> *Diapedesis (passing of blood or any constituents, especially*
>> *erythrocytes, through intact blood vessel walls)*
>
> *Monitor*

Diapedesis is a rare phenomenon, usually quite dangerous. Blood oozes through the blood vessel walls. It can be caused by high blood pressure, or, oddly enough, very low blood pressure.

Maria Wilson, senior **selectwoman** on the Nantucket Town Council, was being **monitored** for intravessel bleeding when the rest of the council arrived at her semi-private room at Constance Woodburn Memorial Hospital in Boston. They'd taken the Woods Hole auto ferry and piled into Jessie Meyers' old Mercedes and driven up to Boston on the turnpike.

Maria looked as if her blood had leapt out of her capillaries and into the interstices of organs and skin. Her cheeks were in a high flush as if suffused with the maverick blood.

"Will you please leave me alone?" she exclaimed as they came piling in the door of her room. Her roommate was hooked up to a number of gadgets that involved tubes containing liquids at various stages of emptying. The roommate delicately pulled her blanket up over the tubes and tactfully tilted her chin up toward the monitor of her television set.

"We have to know how you plan to vote." George Hemphill swayed over her bed, standing lightly on the toe of his one foot.

Words: *Gallfly (a gall wasp that deposits its eggs in plants, causing*
>> *the formation of galls—a swelling of plant tissue—in which*
>> *the larvae feed)*
>
> *Private treaty*
>
> *Gig (a light two-wheeled one-horse carriage)*

I've made a **private treaty** with the **gallfly**—to stop pestering the horse in exchange for coming under my bell jar so I can bring it to the greenhouse and let it cavort among the tropical plants. It can lay its eggs on the undersides of giant orchid leaves or drop from them like pearls up the stems.

My plants are strong. They can harbor the life of the baby gallflies, but the horse is weak. That's why it's so sad, hitched to a **gig**, that it no longer answers even to the flick of the whip and it has forgotten its name. I can't allow a fly to torment its eyes. Let the sad horse die in peace.

Words: *Agnus Dei (Lamb of God—a liturgical prayer addressed*
      to Christ as savior. An image of a lamb with a halo and
      a banner and cross, used as a symbol of Christ.)
      Coverage
      Desktop

The children build a Lamb of God in the snow. I draw the scene on a large sheet of paper that serves as a blotter on my **desktop**. Why do we need blotters anymore? I've bought an ink pen to justify it. I hate to have anything in my house that has no use. The children are building the lamb standing up. The snow is that deep. It takes shape a little at a time outside my window. Their padded knees are wet from kneeling in the snow. Earlier there was lightning and thunder. Then the rain fell down white and didn't stop. It's still falling, but they couldn't wait, and they got dressed and ran out into it. Two inches, three inches, five, six. It's **covered** the trees, the roofs, the hats and scarves of the children. They need a halo. They take the idea for it from the curled branch of the forsythia bush bent under the snow. They snap it off and twist it end to end in a circle, tie it with a loose thread from the girl's red scarf. The ears of the lamb hold it on. Another twig—straight, this one— and the red scarf wrapped round it make the banner. **Agnus De**i, the children chant—Agnus Dei, Agnus Dei, Agnus Dei.

Words: *Bereavement*
        Top
        Amazon

A **top** hat, a real one, is very soft. It's made of fur like silk, if it's expensive, and soft wool felt, if cheap. At Halloween the party-goer dons a paper one and imagines he or she looks dapper.

Along the **Amazon**, the **bereaved** English and German gentlemen attend their friends' funerals in the glistening heat. They can barely refrain from tearing off their shirts and swatting at mosquitoes, but they stand erect in morning coats and top hats, out of respect for their countrymen who lie forever silenced by the tips of poisoned arrows. At their backs, somewhere beyond the shipping town, dark angry men with giant underlips laugh sardonically about their poor aim in hitting the one below his ribs and the other below his collar bone. They'd both aimed for the hearts.

Words: *Insignificant*
        Tone
        Burnet (any of a genus of herbs of the rose family)

In tunes of only a few notes, the through line is important. They work like the **tones** of a bagpipe. The tone of bagpipes beyond the hedge row, the pipers march along the cobbles—Clop...Clop...Deliberate steps and the keening sounds echoing off the stones, turning the corner they march toward us solemn. Someone died in ages past and we weep for them now as the brown **roses** droop their heads to the sound. **Insignificant** people—the miller's daughter, the infantryman—but their deaths are exalted on the rose-sweetened air by the keening tone of the bagpipes. Nothing silly in the knees of the plaid-skirted men. The bony knees and sinewy calves.

Words: *Airhead (an area in hostile territory secured usually by airborne troops for further use in bringing in troops and materiel by air)*
      Booster
      Feast

It's as if a carnival were going on at the **airhead**. On the ground, people raising glasses of wine to the air as **booster** rockets send their missiles streaming up toward the planes and their little man-confetti popping out like party umbrellas and floating paper-like to the beach. The drunken entourage doesn't know enough to come out of the rain of sparks and shrapnel that fall around their heads. It's **feast** or famine these days. Too many troops or too few. Today they celebrate the certain defeat of these pesky hornets that invade their shores.

Words: *Indeterminacy*
      Population
      Cybernation (automatic control of a process or operation— as in Manufacturing—by means of computers)

The computer age and all it stands for awash in the **indeterminacy** of the soul. The soul determines nothing anymore. Among the **population** at large, **cybernacy** has replaced it.

The sip of greenness from an ancient tea cup once, the design hand-painted by a forlorn court artist waiting to be betrothed to the son of the master's servant. She is trained in the lightest brush strokes. Since childhood she has practiced how to put the tip of a two-strand brush to ceramic and dot a hundred flourishes on the pictures of a pagoda roof. The pattern has survived for centuries, but she lasted only into the second year of her marriage and died of inactivity and loneliness. She smashed the cups she produced for the master's son's wedding banquet two days before the event and two seconds before she threw herself over the balcony rail on which her cups sat drying. From above, her silk-robed body made a beautiful picture of royal red amidst the fragments of white and blue.

Today the cups come off assembly lines all over the world. Where **overpopulation** threatens to sink us in the mire of underemployment, the process of painting cups is **cybernated** to avoid imperfections and cut labor costs.

PARLANCE

Some Awesome Issues

THE OLDER YOU GET THE MORE changes you see in the language. Awesome. Awesome used to mean "inspiring dread, veneration and wonder." Now it means, "That's nice" or "Okay."

"Credit or debit?"

"Credit."

"Awesome."

Oddly, this doesn't bother me. I've always liked Valley Speak because I like the hyperbole. I know you know what hyperbole means, but just in case, it means exaggeration. You remember "Gag me with a spoon"? I know, they don't say that anymore, but they should. "Gag me with a spoon." That is awesome hyperbole.

The other day I heard a young woman at a deli talking to her friend. She opened a sandwich she'd just bought and she said "There's hardly any spread on this." And her friend said, "Just tell 'em. They would totally add some more." Totally. Awesome hyperbole.

My brother thinks the word "tweak" is an abomination. So naturally, I torment him with it. "Hey, Frankie. Have you tweaked that project of yours yet? Tweaked it just a little? A little tweak here a little tweak there? Don't freak! I'm just sayin'. It could use a little tweak." He covers his ears, goes la la la la la. That's fun.

I don't mind "tweak" at all. I think tweak could be the perfect euphemism for a particular obscenity.

"Hey drive it lady!"

"Yeah? Tweak off, you tweakin' road hog."

"Huh?"

Then ... there's "like." The only time I object to the littering of sentences with the word "like" is when the word is meaningless. "Like" often does have a meaning.: "My teacher is like, 'Stacey, come to class on time,' and I'm like 'I'm *trying*!'" Here, "like" means "to *say*."

Or "Hey Stacey, what time is it?" "It's like 11:30." Here, Stacey isn't *sure* what time it is. She's approximating.

But, "Hey Stacey, what time is it?" "It's like 11:23."

Is it *like* 11:23? Or is it *actually* 11:23? I'm guessing it's actually 11:23.

Or, "Stacy, you want to come over tonight?" "I can't. I'm, like, going to a concert tonight."

Really? Will she stand outside the venue and feel the reverb through her feet? See, that's the use of "like" that I don't like.

But my special word that I abhor ... and I can hardly bring myself to say it ... is ... "Issue. *Issue*!"

Even the current, most up to date Merriam-Webster online dictionary agrees with me—an "issue" is: "a matter that is in dispute between two or more parties." It is not an illness. It is not a condition. It is not a problem.

I have a chronic pain in my 4th toe. I do not have a 4th toe issue. I have a 4th toe pain. Or you could even say I have a 4th toe problem. You could only call it a 4th toe *issue* if I said to my doctor, "I have a pain in my 4th toe," and my doctor said, "No, you don't. There is no such thing as a pain in the 4th toe. Here is the evidence," and he pushes a medical book at me, and I give him *my* evidence. I stick my swollen toe in his face. *That* would be a 4th toe *issue*.

This use of the word "issue" emerged, I think, about fifteen or twenty years ago along with the expression "differently abled." Someone—and I'd love to know who—decided that the perfectly useful words "problem" and "pain" were *just too negative*! So, we got "issue." Gag me with a spoon!

Everybody uses "issue" now—newscasters, presidents, war correspondents. It's standard. I get the magazine *The Week*. It was reported that Justin Bieber collapsed on stage with "breathing issues." Huh. Did Justin fall on the floor in a tantrum because some people in the audience complained, "Hey, you're taking too many breaths!"? And he said, "I'm taking ... exactly ... the right ... number ... of breaths."

Oh, but wait a minute, they reported breathing iss*ues*! Plural. So maybe another part of the audience was yelling, "Breathe more seductively!" and he thought "I'm the *king* of seductive breathing!"

Breathing *issues*.

I, like, totally hate that word.

Mangled Metaphors

AS I BELIEVE I MENTIONED earlier, I listen to a lot of Audio Books. Often bad ones. Bad thrillers, bad mysteries, bad courtroom suspense dramas. I do this because I'm addicted to having someone yammer away at me while I do my exercises or clean the house or try to get to sleep. As long as I'm being told a story, I'll put up with any amount of bad writing.

The main thing that makes bad writing bad is the frequency of bad figures of speech.

Metaphors and similes are supposed to make a description more vivid by comparing one thing to another thing that's similar. For example, "The baby has roses in her cheeks today." It doesn't mean the baby's mouth is stuffed with flowers. It's an association of roses with pinkness. An easily grasped image. And most importantly a compatible one. New born babies—blooming roses. You can see how they go together.

But here's what I heard in a published—I might add successful—novel. The author writes the following: "A whiplash of pain stings my heart. My lungs, like every one of my organs, are made of crushed glass. The shattered pieces cascade like sand down my chest, landing in my stomach."

You know, I very seldom think of sand cascading. Water, maybe. Even rocks. But sand? And was it the whiplash that crushed the glass? Or shattered it? Or whatever?

Further along in the book this same author claims to have a "gnawing ache that's tumbling through my belly."

I'm wondering how that ache can manage to gnaw and tumble at the same time.

"On the back of my neck," this author says, "my single drop of

46

sweat swells into a tidal wave as I start to see the new reality I'm now sitting in."

Why is he just sitting there in that new reality, when a tidal wave of sweat is coming at him? Man, get off your duff and start running.

All three of these dysfunctional literary passages I've just quoted are from a novel published by an established publishing house, though, perhaps, one that no longer employs editors.

A different author writes "Louis was wracked by a deadly cocktail of indecision, apathy, presentiments, even melancholy."

That is some cocktail. Not only full of existential ingredients, but a cocktail that can "wrack" you. Correct me if I'm wrong, but doesn't wrack (or 'rack') literally mean having your limbs pulled out of their sockets and ripped from your torso by pulleys? I just don't see a cocktail quite accomplishing that feat, even figuratively. I think Louis should stay away from cocktails. *Louis*, go on the wagon!

Another best-selling novelist claims "The sun beat down on them like a sky full of heat lamps." I'm having a hard time picturing a sky full of heat lamps, or even a spa full of heat lamps.

Another writer insists that an unsolved problem "still nagged at a corner of my brain like a pesky hangnail."

Do brains have corners? Let's not even mention pesky hangnails.

Even on the radio you hear these bad metaphors. An NPR weather reporter claimed "A mild day is on tap." I'm picturing this reporter bellying up to the bar and ordering that mild day at a local saloon.

An expert, also on NPR, made the following announcement: "Rest assured, the violence level is going to go up." Well, thank you, sir! Now I *can* rest assured.

Language baffles me. Yesterday the cashier at Safeway asked me, "Do you need the receipt at all?" Do I need it at *all*? Do I *partially* need it? Or do I need only part of it? Just the sales tax part maybe? I'm not sure how to answer. So I just say, Yes.

Then there's "Absolutely." "May I bring you your check now, Sir?" "Absolutely." Not just the cost of the appetizer, but the *whole thing*!

Now, I blame us baby boomers for "absolutely." "Absolutely" is the direct descendent of my generation's "great."

"Okay, so I'll meet you at the corner of 5th and Main at noon?" "Great!"

Great? The successful exploration of the Antarctic between 1901 and 1904 without benefit of Goretex or GPS in a three-masted wooden schooner that got trapped in ice for a year. *That* was great.

I was a teacher of English as a Second Language, and we taught our non-native speaker students that if they wanted to speak in the rhythm of North American English, they needed to put stress on what we call content words. For example, if I say, "Do you want to go to a movie tonight?" I could get rid of all the function words—articles, prepositions, auxiliaries, etc.—and you'd still get the gist: Want go movie tonight? But if I get rid of those content words, what remains will convey nothing: Do you to to a?

The content words get strong beats, and the topic gets the highest pitch: Do you WANT to GO to a <u>MOVIE</u> TONIGHT? But if you listen to the radio carefully you'll hear something like this: "This *is* NPR" (Who said it *wasn't*?) Or "it's 77 degrees *in* Des Moines." As opposed to *outside* of Des Moines? Apparently at some point, stressing the word "is" or "in" for no reason whatsoever became a media-speak convention. And all news and weather reporters have to do it or they *absolutely* get fired, thus driving them to drink those bitter existential cocktails filled to the brim with crushed glass.

But Is It English?

I'VE HAD TO ACCEPT THE FACT that *amount* has now replaced the word *number*. ("I couldn't believe the amount of people who were there. At least a thousand!" Gack!) I've gone through the five stages of grief on behalf of "*number*" indicating things countable, as opposed to "*amount*" indicating uncountable things like air and water.

First, I went through Denial (No, no, it must have been a slip of the tongue!); Anger (Idiots! Do you picture those thousand people as a huge mound of undifferentiated flesh?); Bargaining (Look, I'll show you any ESL textbook so you can understand the difference between amount and number. How about that?); Depression (I'll never again hear the language I taught so conscientiously); Acceptance (Language changes. If the meaning is clear, who cares? Get *over* it.)

Speaking of ambiguous quantities, I heard on the radio: "a little bit of the elections are …" (A little part of each election? A few of the elections?)

Then there are the following choices that assault my ears like chalk squeaking on a blackboard: "It's a strange phenomena." (Both singular and plural at the same time? That *would* be strange.), "Ekcetera" (Don't get me started.) "A song was being sang." (Ditto.)

This one assaults my *eyes*: "It just get's worse." (Ban the inexplicable apostrophe!)

A U.S. legislator used the phrase "… where it's at." I cringed, revealing to myself the snob that I am. It's an expression whose meaning is perfectly clear, so there's no reason to get exercised over it. It's standard everywhere now, but it still grates on this old woman's nerves.

Regarding the composer Richard Wagner, I heard, "… after him and his wife's third child was born—" On Facebook: "20 years!! Today is Jeff and I's wedding anniversary!" And the classic "Me and the rest of the group went to ..." (Would you say, "Me went to ..."?) Also, the overcorrection: "The story is about he and I." ("About" is a *preposition*. It takes an *object* pronoun. Would you say, "The story is about he"? or "The story is about I"?)

And what about dazzlingly absurd but inadvertent exaggerations? On public radio this morning, talking about the European regulation set to take effect there soon—i.e. electronic gadgets must all use the same kind of connector in their charging devices—"The change would save the average user $250,000,000 a year." (The average European is richer than I'd realized!)

Or the obfuscating use of euphemisms: A sign posted on the doors to the swimming pool: "Due to clarity issues, pool closed." (Just *say* it: The pool is as murky as a swamp.)

Cutesy words:

"Guesstimate." What is a guesstimate? Is it a guess or is it an estimate? And more to the point, is there a reason for this word to exist? I'm guessing that it exists to sound cute. If the world's average temperature rises by 3 degrees Celsius by the middle of the next century, as much as 75% of the Amazon rain forest will be destroyed. That's an estimate. My hydrangeas didn't bloom so well this year. Maybe because of the drought. I don't know. It's a guess.

And I estimate that by the year 2030 the words guess and estimate will have become extinct. A pity.

Then there's "At first blush."

"At first blush." What does this mean? If it means "at first," why not say, "at first"? The only situation in which "At first *blush*" might make sense to me is "At first blush I didn't care for spicy food, but now I enjoy it." By this I mean that the *first* time I ate a jalapeño enchilada, my face got beet red and sweat dropped onto the tortilla chips. I didn't like this. Later, I came to enjoy jalapeño enchiladas even though they still made me flush to the roots and sweat like a stevedore.

But that's not how the expression "at first blush" is used.

For example: "At first blush the house looks rather small, but when you go inside, you find it's quite roomy." What I want to know is why anyone would blush about misjudging the size of a house? Furthermore, if you were so oversensitive as to blush at this minor mistake, why blush *at first*, before you discovered you were wrong?

Where did this expression come from? And why did whoever first say it think "At first" was just not good enough, it needed embellishment? I don't know. Maybe, again, to sound cute? But, that's just a guesstimate. (Oops, I've just been informed that the word "blush" is derived from an Old English word meaning "glimpse." So apparently the expression "at first blush" has a perfectly logical antecedent. I stand corrected. But it still sounds silly to me.)

Misplaced modifiers are always good for a laugh. Why should we care if a modifier dangles? Well, things that dangle, aren't they just a little bit goofy? Those dangly bits? I mean, can you take seriously a statement like, "This had long been a fear of mine, that my wallet will be stolen while trying on new clothes." (Does my wallet need new clothes?) Or "Patricia's story began as a little girl in Indiana." (Can a story be a little girl?)

"We organized groups to go out to vaccinate people twice a week." (Their arms must get so sore!) "As a mom, rising healthcare costs are a big concern." (Are rising health care costs classified as moms these days?)

New York Times: As a child, the beach was uncomplicated. (So the beach's childhood was serene and simple until it reached its late teens when the beach's parents divorced and started competing for its affections. The waves would encroach on the beach grass's rights, and the sand would always be caught in the middle.)

"Approaching twenty-three, my favorite activity has become being in bed by seven to watch this show." (That favorite activity has been old enough to vote for the last five years and buy beer for the last two. But it's not so old as to retire at seven in front of the tube on a regular basis.)

But if you want to dangle your modifier, go ahead, let it hang there.

As you may imagine, my least or most (depending on how you look at it) favorite misunderstanding of a word is *literally*. For the depths of my outrage, see the next chapter, "Literally."

What else? Oh yes, I always enjoy an accidental insult:

In a retirement residence weekly memo: "Come to the Art Room on Saturday to meet the art teacher and some of her students while enjoying some of their art." (Warning: you might not enjoy *all* of their art.)

And clichés like this: He comes by his talent honestly. (What does this even mean? Is dishonest talent a thing?)

Completely inexplicable is the Yeah-no reply:

> A: I know you're busy this morning, maybe you need more time to get ready.
> B: Yeah, no, I'll be ready.

> Survivor: So many people lost everything.
> Newscaster: Yeah, no, it's hard to see people who've lost so much.

And the "is is" redundancy: "The fact is is that …" "The truth is is that …" "The thing is is that …"

But few language gaffes are quite so diverting as a headline gone wrong—

Headline in today's *Press Citizen*: "JUDGE: JASPER COUNTY'S VICIOUS ANIMAL ORDINANCE UNCONSTITUTIONAL"

(Which is vicious, the animal or the ordinance? If the latter, boy, that's mighty biased reportage. The article isn't even on the Op Ed page!)

A caption for a Meidas Touch YouTube video: "Trump Suffers Massive Issues in Awful Detroit Speech." (How do you suffer an issue?)

Oh yeah, my beef with "issue." (See earlier chapter: "Some Awesome Issues")

"He's having issues with his brother-in-law." (Disagreements? Murderous impulses? Annoyance that the brother-in-law keeps borrowing his car? Disapproval of the brother-in-law's toupee?) It's a portmanteau word meaning anything you want it to. Why specify?)

Other portmanteaus:

Process [verb] "It must have been hard to process all you were going through." (Cope with? Understand? Get over? React to? ...)

Paradigm [noun]: "He's society's paradigm for the perfect male." (Is there a reason why you'd choose "paradigm" over *model, pattern, example, standard, prototype, ideal, criterion, pattern, guideline, principle, embodiment, manifestation, role model, or idea*?) ...

And don't get me started on "paradigm *shift*." Tim Carter, *Chicago Tribune*, 5 May 2023: "... the paradigm shift in residential plumbing happened with PEX tubing." (Are the words "major change" not highfalutin' enough for residential plumbing?)

What about the brain glitch sound reversal—the old gray matter champing at the bit to get on with the sentence before a thought is finished. Always good for a laugh:

David Pakman talking about the language glitches in J.D. Vance's speech: "We were told he would be really clystal crear in his speech" (crystal clear) A meta reproval!

"Pre D thinking" (3D printing) and "I've been having mental problems ..." (medical and dental problems). I confess that these two came directly from my brain—mental problems indeed!

Right-wing newscaster: "If you combine Bernie Warr—" (If you combine Bernie Sanders and Elizabeth Warren ...). Especially funny because that's what this newscaster just did. Meta, again!

Barack Obama in his speech at the 2024 DNC. "We've all got our blah—" (We've all got our blind spots.) It would have been especially funny if he hadn't caught himself before saying, We've all got our blond spites.

Doug Emhoff's speech at the DNC convention: "I still get to be a lawyer by teaching stordents—" (… by teaching students at Georgetown Law School.) Where did those stordents come from? Mars?

My thought about how I tripped in the parking garage and face-planted onto a "concrete barking pumper." (parking bumper) A barking pumper might have left less of a bruise.

Me noticing the building going up across the street: "It looks like a Froynk Lade Wright." (the architect)

Typos: also good for a laugh.

An email to a friend: "Geetings, Julia" [Greetings]

Email to another friend: "What's the latest on your state of ming?" [retyped it:] "What's the latest on your state of mine?" [retyped it:]"What's the latest on you state o mind?" [Finally get it right:] "What's the latest on your state of mind?" [A little ironic that I'm asking about *her* state of mind]

"He's a guy who lives on my floot." [floor] What is it like to live on a floot? Is it something that floats, like a houseboot? [Oops—house-*boat*]. [You have to be very small to live on a houseboot.]

"I got some goo tips from your list of uplifting things." [I got some good tips] "Uplists are a little gooey" [I meant to say Uplifts] [So then I typed]: ("I meant to say Uplefts.") [I ended that last parenthetical statement with ( ) instead of)] [I started to type penthetical instead of parenthetical and I typed "s tatement in that last sentence."] "I got some good tips from your short list of uplighting things." [uplifting] [But maybe "uplighting is also apt.] Will this never end?

"I was wearing a wood beret" [wool] [Not warm, and certainly not comfortable.]

If you are a non-native speaker, learning English vocabulary will be a walk in the park compared to learning the subtleties of English stress and intonation.

We can say, "We're going to be pretty late," "It's pretty tasty," "He's pretty homely," even, "She's pretty pretty."

But what does "pretty" mean anyway? It depends on the stress and intonation.

<pre>
          book   go-
That   was pretty   od. (pretty = quite)
</pre>

<pre>
                pret-   od.
That book was   ty go-   (pretty = somewhat)
</pre>

So ...

<pre>
       wo-   pret-
That   man was pretty   ty. (pretty = quite pretty)
</pre>

<pre>
                pret-   ty.
That woman was   ty pret-   (pretty = somewhat pretty)
</pre>

I was working a crossword puzzle. A clue: "Don't look at me!" The answer: "*I* didn't do it." I.e.

"Don't look at ME.

But I had read it with the following intonation in mind:

<pre>
        LOOK
" Don't   at me!" (I hate being looked at.)
</pre>

Finally, last but not least, irregular verb forms:

Present	Past	
Keep	(not keeped)	but kept
Creep	creeped	and crept
Peep	peeped	but not pept
Leave	(not leaved)	but left

Present	Past	
Believe	believed	but not beleft
Dream	dreamed	and dreamt
Seem	seemed	but not semt
Kneel	kneeled	and knelt
Feel	(not feeled)	but felt
Lend	(not lended)	but lent
End	ended	but not ent

Why? Why not?

Literally

BLACK WOMEN AT HARVARD LAW SCHOOL reflect on Ketanji Brown Jackson: "We are literally walking in her shoes." (Kind of uncomfortable for Ketanji. But maybe she is an Imelda Marcos type of woman with a huge closet full of shoes and the law students sneak into her house to walk in them.)

From Adam Mockler on his podcast re Elon kotowing to Trump: "[Elon Musk] literally dropped to his knees and actually begged." (Really? Did he? Hard to imagine.)

From Trump: "You saw what happened to some of the witnesses who were on our side? They were literally crucified by this man ..." (My, that must have been gory. I'm impressed, though, that the man went to the considerable trouble of building those crosses. To say nothing of hoisting them up. He had to have had help.)

"Republicans are having a literal meltdown ..." (I'd love to see that. Is it like a tuna melt?)

Or "Man, I am literally dead!" (Whoa! Back off, zombie!)

A guy on the radio reminisces about his old New York neighborhood. He claims, "The trees literally hugged the brownstone apartments."

I have news for you, sir. No, they didn't. If they had literally hugged the brownstones, they would have sprouted human arms, which extended all the way around the whole building and pulled those brownstones up against the trunks. Literally doesn't mean "like" or "almost." It means "in actual fact." There's a word for how the trees were hugging those buildings. The word is "figuratively." But you can just say the trees hugged the buildings. We get it.

Sometimes I get flak for complaining about this misuse of *literally*. I don't *literally* get flak. If I *literally* got flak, I would be in the hospital with actual shrapnel wounds. The figurative flak I get is this: Don't be such a language snob! Words *change*! There's hardly a word in English that means exactly what it meant a hundred years ago! That's the *nature* of *language*. Get with the program!

Yes, I know. I know. Language changes. But, I'm sorry, there are some words that deserve better treatment. "Literally" has a precise meaning, which is: "Hey, you might have trouble believing this, because it's so unexpected, but here's what, in actual fact, happened!"

That's a highly specific, multi-layered meaning packed into one beautiful internally alliterative word (those two lovely "l" sounds). Shouldn't we protect that meaning from extinction? From being turned into its opposite?

All other words?—fine, let them be turned on their heads. But leave "literally" alone! I do not want "literally" made a laughing stock on the language playground with sentences like: "You literally go into the woods and forage for granola." (From an interview on NPR.)

I don't want to hear "[My grandma] could literally snore the paint off the wall."

Or "If there's one thing I wish everyone could have growing up, it would be a dad with eyes like his. He could literally hug you with them." (That came from the memoir of a state senator. Senator, I'm sorry, but that is just a gruesome image.)

"Literally" should not mean "figuratively." It's like saying, "I had a huge lunch, so I'm extremely hungry." Hey, what's the problem? I'm just making "huge" mean "tiny." It's my *right*, you fussy, self-righteous language purist.

Last example: "My boss is literally an ass." (You are employed by a long-eared hairy quadruped who says "Hee haw"? That literally blows me away!)

Blessed

A TORNADO PASSED THROUGH my town this week. A whole lot of people claimed to be "blessed" to have their houses spared.

The tornado flattens your next door neighbor's house but leaves yours with a few shingles missing. Because you were blessed? How does blessing come into it? If by blessed you mean you were extraordinarily lucky, why not say so? Man, we were so lucky! That tornado came within six inches of our house.

If you mean that an omniscient, omnipresent, omnipotent supernatural deity smiled on you that day, then why did that deity frown on your next door neighbors, who attended the same church as you and gave generously to the poor and took loving care of their elderly parents and had finally paid off their mortgage?

In the Oklahoma bombing, children died. Others, who were "blessed," didn't. Did a deity decide those other children were expendable because they forgot to put their nickel in the collection box? Or they said a naughty word on the playground? Is that why they weren't blessed?

Or are you saying those children got scooped up to heaven early, so they were actually twice as blessed as yours, and their parents should be thankful that their little ones are up there happily playing in celestial sandboxes? Do you wish your children had been so doubly blessed rather than only singly blessed?

Darkness

J.D. Vance (before seeing what side his bread was buttered on):
"[Trump's] leading the white working class to a very dark place."

WHAT IF YOUR SKIN IS DARK? What does this persistently negative characterization of darkness say to you?

"These were dark times." "I was overwhelmed by dark thoughts." "He was the black sheep." "I was in a black mood." "He had a dark purpose." "It had a darker meaning." "It was blackmail." "They committed dark deeds." "I got blacklisted, blackballed." "She had a dark secret." "They blackened my name." "It was a black mark against her." "The teacher gave me a black look."

But could you have said these were *grim* times? Were you overwhelmed with *pessimism*? He was the *family outcast*? You were *depressed*? *Cheesed off*? Did he have an *evil* purpose? Did it have a *less benign* meaning? Was it *extortion*? Did they commit *dirty* deeds? Did you get *banned*? Did she have a *disreputable* secret? Did they *ruin your reputation*? Was it a *stain* on her character? Did the teacher *scowl* at you?

Apart from the hurtful association of darkness with all things bad (all but a few—"in the black" is a rare exception), it's a lazy use of vocabulary. Pick up a thesaurus, already. (If you're too modern to open the *pages* of a thesaurus, just type "dark synonym" in the google search box. It practically does the work *for* you.)

Seventy percent of the world's population have melanin-rich skin. Seventy-five to eighty-five percent have dark hair. And what about all the happy, necessary and beautiful aspects of darkness?

To name a few:

The richest, most fertile soil
Nighttime, bringing deep sleep
Storm clouds before a needed rain
The lustrous hair color of those with raven locks
The lustrous flesh color of those with ebony skin
The wondrous night sky and outer space beyond
The deep ocean, full of endless, timeless mystery
Beaches of fine black volcanic sand, soft under the feet
The black belt, signifying the highest rank in the martial arts
Black swans, cats, horses, panthers, pandas, penguins, seals
Crows, grackles, red-winged blackbirds, starlings, cormorants, swifts
Graphite—the useful mineral in electric vehicles' battery anodes
and in the humble pencil
Raisins, figs, dates, prunes, blackberries, currants, brownies, caviar,
soy sauce, vanilla, pepper, poppy seeds, balsamic vinegar, caviar,
eggplant, walnuts, black beans, black olives, black pepper, black
bread, black truffles, almonds, walnuts, hazelnuts, peanuts
Brisket, blackened shrimp, black rice, brown rice
Tea, Coffee
Chocolate

And what about negative *white* things: maggots, mold, fungus, pus, tapeworms, cataracts, spoiled milk, scars, bird poop, cocaine, blizzards, hail, white supremacy, Ku Klux Klan robes, strep throat, phlegm, (smelly) gym socks, ashen and pasty complexions due to ill health or shock, the cadavers of dead white people …

Let's suppose the tables were turned:

It was a white day when that evil man came into our lives; I was overwhelmed by white thoughts of suicide and revenge; He had a white purpose, known only to his henchmen; She harbored a terrible, white secret; After my shameful behavior, I was whiteballed, from my club and white-listed by my political party; They whitened my name and cast me out; I was the white sheep of my family.

Etc.

All of which begs the question: Are we white people simply jealous?

TRUTH TO POWER

Bad News Good News

ELECTION
> Tuesday, 11-8-16:
>> Trump elected president.

AFFLICTION
> Wednesday, 11-9-16:
>> I come down with pneumonia. Coincidence?

ELATION
> Tuesday, 11-3-20:
>> Biden elected president.

CONVICTION
> Thursday, 5-30-24:
>> Trump found guilty on all 34 counts!! Oh happy day!
>
> Friday, 5-31-24:
>> 2:30 a.m. Woke from great dream! A young Judge Juan Merchan without the white in his hair or the black-framed glasses. Remember him? The judge who presided over Trump's conviction? Handsome guy? We are walking down a path together. Gazing into each other's eyes.
>
> Sunday, 6-2-24:
>> 4:15 a.m. Another romantic dream early this morning! (Thank you, Trump trial jurors!)
>
> Thursday, 6-6-24:
>> 3:10 a.m. Still another euphoric dream! (Three in the last week since the Trump verdict)

DERELICTION

Monday, 7-1-24:

Supreme Court grants Trump immunity from criminal prosecution.

PREDICTION

Monday, 11-4-24

The election will be close, but she will win.

CONNIPTION

Tuesday, 11-5-24:

He wins the election.

DEFECTION

That does it. I'm moving to Canada. (But will they take Americans so stupid that they allowed this to happen?)

Humility

hum•ble /həm•b(ə)l
verb: lower (someone) in dignity or importance
adjective: 1) having or showing a modest or low estimate of one's own importance 2) of low social, administrative, or political rank 3a) expressing, reflecting or offered in a spirit of deference or submission 3b) not costly or luxurious

One thing you can count on from the man who lives in the Florida White House is that he never, under any circumstances, applies the word "humble" or "humbled" to himself. Though his vocabulary is severely limited, he seems to intuit the true meaning of the word and doesn't even use it with the false humility of a person acknowledging a high honor by declaring: "I am deeply humbled by this award."

Lowering the Decibels
(A performance piece)

IN THESE TROUBLING TIMES, it's important to maintain a calm, civil tone in our political discourse and try to resist the temptation to engage in shrill shouting matches. We need to lower the decibel level and stick to thoughtful, quiet expressions of opinion. Something like this:

[Spoken throughout with quiet restraint:]

>You puffed up money-grubbing jackass,
>   you disgusting parasite.
>Who do you think you are?
>Going to cut taxes for the rich, are you?
>*Tell* us that's going to boost the economy,
>   you sneaky, chiseling fraud.
>Try filling your *own* bathtub on a trickle,
>   you heartless corrupt opportunist.
>Who pays for your six-figure three per week
>   golf club getaways?
>Taxpayers? The poor? The disabled?
>What would your budget look like
>   if you wrote it with a pen between
>   *your* teeth, you greedy double-dealing thug?
>
>So you want to build a wall to keep out the Mexicans.
>Really? And where are you going to cut the door
>   to let in your maids, your busboys,
>   and your gardeners?
>It seems you got a bum rap for racism.

Your best friends are people of color.
As long as the color is orange
    and comes from a tanning bed.

"Oh, look at my African American over there!
Look at him. Are you the greatest? A fan of mine.
Great guy!" You really said that. And women.
They exist for your groping pleasure, do they?
How did your mental maturity get stuck way back in
    Junior High, you sniggering, sleazy, scumball?

Gotta show everyone how tough you are, you
    vicious schoolyard bully?
Nuke countries you can't even find on a map, you
    war-mongering goon?
Hey, you don't *need* bombs.
Forget about first strike capability.
Just send them an infantile three a.m. tweet.
They'll be laughing so hard they won't
    be able to strike back.
Your creepy face could be the ultimate
    defense of America.

And no need to read those pesky intelligence reports.
You have to actually have intelligence to understand them.
Do you even know what the Constitution is, you
    ignorant buffoon?
    Or first amendment rights? Or conflicts of interest?
Or are phrases of more than two words just too hard?

Let me break it down for you.
Free speech ... good, free religion ... good,
    free press ... tremendous.

Cheating … bad. Stealing … bad. Lying … nasty.
Or is that still too complex for a man
    Who's nothing but a made for TV special?

What are you going to do when the ice caps melt
    and your towers fall into the flood, you
    short-sighted, mindless incompetent?
Charter a rocket to the moon?
Load up your billionaire cronies, two by two?
Maybe even bring along the wives and kids
    if there's enough space?

Is there anyone in the world who thinks
    you're fit to lead this country,
    you conniving swindler?
Oh yes, Vladimir Putin, and probably Kim Jung-un,
    if he gave it some thought—
    he likes people who remind him of himself.

So, congratulations, Sir.
You have now joined the ranks of Sociopaths in Chief.

So you see, a lot can be expressed without the need to shout.

Why I Am a Supporter

WHY DO I SUPPORT DONALD TRUMP? Well, this is my *opinion*, but everyone tells me I have great opinions. They all say my opinions are incredible. The best opinions of anyone they know.

I support him because ... he ... cares about the little guy. You wouldn't believe how much he cares about the little guy. He cares more about the little guy than any other president, ever. It's tremendous how much he cares, considering how much money he has. I mean, he has more money than anyone. You don't have to trust me on that. He says so himself. And that much money means you're smart. So you know he's the smartest president there ever was.

But those aren't the only reasons I support him. I could name a hundred reasons, a thousand reasons, like ... he ... *fixes* things! Anything that's broken in this country, he'll fix it. That's what I appreciate about him because I know what it's like to see broken things and want to fix them. Everyone who knows me knows I don't let anything sit around broken. They say I'll fix it before other people even *notice* it's broken. People say I can fix something *while* it's breaking. I don't know about that. Maybe. *I'm* not going to say it. But that's what people say.

So he's tremendous about fixing things. He's already fixed more things than *all* the previous administrations going back to ... going all the way back. What things? *You* know what they are. I don't have to go into it.

Another reason ... He tells it like it is. He says what's on his mind. *Whatever's* on his mind. All these politicians, you have no idea what they're thinking. Everything *he's* thinking you know about it because he tells you. And it's 100% true. So much truth. I'm like that. If I think someone's a loser, I'll say, "You're a loser." And you wouldn't believe how much they respect me for that.

If it was up to me, I would just let him say what he wants to say, do what he wants to do. He wants incredibly good laws. The best laws. Why should he have to beg the politicians—Congress or whatever—to pass good laws? It takes them forever to come up with—. Like money for the Wall. That should be in the Constitution. ... I've been down to Arizona, New Mexico. Believe me it's *dry*. They'll be having those forest fires again. And whose fault is that? Bad hombres and no one raking the forests like they're supposed to. That's sad.

But why do we even need a constitution if it's full of bad laws—. Like ... the Press ... NATO ... wildlife. Those millions of regulations ... oh, and what's the big deal about his tax returns? Talk about a witch h—...

You know what? People don't like to hear it, but I'll be honest with you, if it's between the way things were before and him being king, I'd say king. This country needs a strong man. Kick the Islams out and the liberals and other undesirables. Send them down to Puerto Rico if they're so—no, *farther* out, like an island in the middle of the Pacific Ocean. An island.

I went to Barbados one time. They have great rum there, I'm telling you. Those little umbrellas. Wait, is that with rum, or ... Margaritas? No, that's salt. Believe me, an island would not be a punishment. Only thing is ... if you bring rum back from Barbados you have to pay a customs fee. They search your luggage. There are ways *around* that. You just have to know someone. Customs! *There's* a scam he'll fix.

So, those are just a few of the millions of reasons why I support Donald Trump.

The Daughters and the Dictators

NO ONE SHOULD HAVE BEEN surprised at how things turned out. It makes me think of that Chinese fable about the guy whose horse ran away. All his neighbors said, Oh too bad, how unfortunate. And the guy just looked unconcerned and said, *Maybe.* (Or did he say, *You never know what will happen?* Anyway, same idea.) The next day, the horse comes back with seven wild horses and all the neighbors said, Wow. That's fantastic. How lucky! And the guy says *Maybe.* Then the day after that, his son is trying to ride one of the horses and falls off and breaks his leg, and the neighb— Well, you get the idea.

That's what I mean about how things turned out. Your generation wasn't even born yet, so it doesn't mean as much to you, but we were all crushed by the results. One party (and not the benevolent, humanitarian one) got control of all branches of government, in perpetuity, or so we thought.

None of us could even talk about it for the first weeks. It was the end of the world as we knew it. There seemed to be no light at the end of the tunnel, or even an end *to* the tunnel. It was like 1933 Germany all over again. Were we now going to join up with the other authoritarian powers and be part of an Axis, while the Allies had to mobilize to take us down before we destroyed the planet? *Us?*

Jeez, it was disorienting.

He was a tyrant the way a two-year-old is a tyrant—*Me! My! Mine! Gimme! Gimme! Gimme!*—and as ignorant as a two-year-old (or maybe a six-year-old, I don't want to exaggerate). His criterion for trusting tyrants from other countries was "He *likes* me."

It seemed as if, however you looked at it, there was no way out except through a kind of cataclysm even though the guy was getting far up there in age and looked like an apoplectic walrus and some people were hoping he would just croak off on his own. Wishful thinking.

Maybe.

What actually happened was beyond imagining.

It began with an interview on his once favorite news channel. He'd soured on that channel since they'd allowed his political opponent and other critics to be interviewed and "get away with murder." But he could still rely on this particular interviewer, who, if she hadn't been almost twenty years older than his daughter, could have passed for the daughter's twin—same shaved nose, plumped-up lips, raccoon eyes and bleach-blonde hair.

(Just as an aside, I think the very small, distinctive bend to the nose his daughter had been born with—you can detect it if you look closely at early photos—and the slight, healthy-looking roundness to her cheeks had gotten tweaked when she was a teenager—at her father's insistence?—so that now her nose was straight as an arrow and her cheekbones as prominent as an anorexic's. It would be likely that he failed to pay the surgeon. Why pay? The new face couldn't be repo'ed.)

The interview started out routinely enough—father and daughter sitting side by side on a sofa in front of a live audience while the interviewer tossed them a few softball questions. She asked what his daughter had been like as a teenager. Had she been rebellious?

He gave his closed-lip grimace that was meant to stand in for a smile and said, "Her mother might have found her rebellious, but *I like 'em* spicy."

And the daughter just gazed at him for a moment—fondly, it *seemed*—then reached into the Versace bag by her side, drew out a pink designer pistol, and shot him point blank in the face.

Yeah. Shot him in the face. And after she returned the gun to her bag, she read what I guess could be called a manifesto, detailing the sexual molestation she'd suffered at his hands since childhood, none of which should have surprised anyone who'd heard all his cringe-worthy public comments about her sexual attractiveness every chance he got.

The guy was incapable of holding back. He was quoted in a famous arts and entertainment magazine, saying: "Yeah, she's really something … If I weren't happily married and, you know, her father—"

Can you imagine this?

On mainstream TV he said, "If she weren't my daughter, I might be dating her." On a talk show on his preferred cable channel, the two of them were asked: "What's your favorite thing you have in common?" The daughter says, "Either real estate or golf." The tyrant says, "Well, I was going to say sex, but I can't say that here."

So, three bullets to the face.

Wow. Great news!

But … what would happen to the daughter? Was she going to rot in prison for the rest of her life? After doing the world this big favor?

Maybe. But you never know what will happen.

In court, her stepmother gave her a glowing character reference. And the manifesto got read out. *That* made an impression on the jury. You could see it in their eyes. Plus, there was that ominous note she produced. Two days before the murder she got a note from her father, telling her to send her thirteen-year-old daughter to his compound down in Florida so she could "get more intimately acquainted with grandpa." I mean, anyone in her shoes would have freaked out.

And, boy, her defense team covered all the bases. Showed the jury that packing a pistol didn't prove premeditation since she always carried the gun for protection. And they had a psychologist testifying that the comment "I *like* 'em spicy" triggered her trauma (*literally* triggered it!), so her lawyers could go with the "acting in the moment" defense. The judge reduced that first degree murder charge to voluntary manslaughter!

She was out in two years. They say she'd done "good time" in there. Tutoring inmates, teaching fashion design, learning how the other half lives.

So we celebrated. It was all good.

Maybe.

Our celebration was brief. We'd forgotten the problem of succession. Out of the frying pan, into the fire.

The next guy in line—second in command to tyrant #1—was as racist, sexist and self-aggrandizing as the other tyrant, if slightly more literate. He thought the only woman worthy of citizenship was one who popped out babies while lying complacently under the boot heel of a husband. (Not an easy feat.)

Big trouble.

Maybe.

After #1's death, tyrant #2 moved into the residence and in the first week held an intimate dinner party in the family dining room for the richest man in the world, who had supported #1. While #2 and his wife were wining and dining this character, the seven-year-old and four-year old sons were in their room playing the banned video game "Active Shooter®," of which the seven-year old had managed to find a pirated copy online.

The three-year-old daughter had been fed Spaghetti-Os® in the family kitchen by the nanny, who promised to give her a cookie if she was a good girl and cleaned her plate, which she did.

The nanny stepped out of the kitchen for a moment to go to the adjoining bathroom, leaving the three-year-old safely under the table with Atlas, the family's gentle German shepherd.

The little girl must have thought that the nanny had forgotten her promise. She crawled from under the table, pushed a kitchen chair over to the cabinet which she knew contained the cookie jar, climbed from the chair to the counter, stood, and slid open the cupboard door. She looked up at the canister just out of reach on a top shelf, tried to grasp it, and in so doing knocked an object off the shelf. It was a loaded 9mm Glock 19 handgun, which was stopped mid-fall when its trigger caught on a cup hook.

At this moment #2 came into the kitchen to ask the nanny to bring the little girl to the dining room in order to show her off to the billionaire, who, himself, had at least twelve children that we knew of. The bullet caught #2 square in the chest—the left side of his chest, to be exact. He died before he hit the floor.

At the sound of the gunshot, #2's wife and the billionaire came running into the kitchen (the nanny didn't hear the shot over the sounds of the flushing toilet and water running in the sink, and took her time coming back). The mother whisked the child away before she could fully grasp and be traumatized by the scene.

It was established that #2 had quite a quantity and variety of loaded handguns stashed around the residence, despite the presence of his two little boys. This was not surprising, given his position on the Second Amendment. (Later, the mother took the children to her parents' house, and they all moved back to their native India, where there were only five civilian firearms per one hundred people.)

After the January 6 insurrection back in 2020, the D.C. police and F.B.I. had become obsessively conscientious and thorough in their investigations, and they agreed unanimously that the only fingerprints on the gun were #2's own prints and the little girl's (along with a smear of spaghetti sauce), so it was definitively confirmed that the event was accidental and not part of a Deep State Democratic assassination conspiracy.

Whew! A sigh of relief.

Maybe.

The succession problem wasn't over.

Tyrant #3 was next in line, having presided over one of the houses of government, and controlled which bills could and could not be brought to the floor. He had a fervent desire to turn the country into a "Christian" theocracy where women's rights—*all* rights, for that matter—boiled down to this: the duty to worship one particular male god with the correct evangelical credentials. The idea that some people might not worship *any* god? Unthinkable.

#3's grown daughters were twenty-three and twenty-one. When the older daughter was thirteen, #3 took her to a "Purity Ball," a rite intended to prevent a young girl from thinking, knowing or hearing about any aspect of sex whatsoever or inspiring sexual thoughts in boys or men by her dress, her walk, her talk or anything else about her, and to commit her to abstaining from dating.

At the ball, the father places a "purity ring" on the girl's finger, which she is to wear until her husband (on the assumption that she *will* get married) replaces it with a wedding ring. I.e., the ownership of her body and her sexuality passes from father to husband, with whom she has a "Covenant Marriage," which makes divorce virtually impossible without the couple being condemned to hell for eternity.

Girls attend the Purity Ball in white gowns similar to wedding dresses and are accompanied by their fathers in black tuxedos. The father attaches a corsage to the daughter's wrist and waltzes with her as if they are on a prom date or at their own wedding. The high point of the evening is her "Purity Vow." She reads and signs a pledge "to make a commitment to God, myself, my family, my friends, my future husband and my future children to a lifetime of purity including sexual purity." Father and daughter look into each other's eyes while she makes this pledge.

Thus, the girl so "protected" is deeply sexualized by her father, in the creepiest way possible.

Meanwhile, both of #3's daughters had been steeped in Biblical lore from early childhood. #3 believed the Bible was inerrant despite its massive number of inconsistencies. When asked in an interview what his world view was, he said, "Well, go pick up a Bible off your shelf and read it. That's my world view."

Inevitably the daughters were exposed to Chapter 19 of Genesis, the first book of the Old Testament, and were grossed out by the story of Lot's daughters.

Two of God's angels showed up at the town of Sodom, where Lot invited them to his house for a bunch of hospitality. The men of

Sodom (*all* the men—old and young!) surrounded Lot's house and demanded he send the angels out so the men could have the pleasure of raping angels. Lot was horrified. God's precious angels debauched by a lascivious mob? For heaven's sake, they were his guests! "I have two virgin daughters," he said. "Take them instead." "All *right!*" said the mob. And the daughters were brought forth. (I'm not making this up. Read the book.)

God punished the Sodomites (excepting Lot, who had protected His angels). The Lord destroyed Sodom (and Gomorrah, thirteen miles away—but what did *they* do?!) and annihilated the men, so that when the daughters got old enough to get pregnant (presumably they'd been children when the mob "knew" them), there were no men left except their own father to impregnate them, thus making it impossible to preserve their father's seed. So, Bob's your uncle!—they got their father drunk and raped him, thereby starting the lineage of Moabites and Ammonites.

Okay, so you can kind of see why #3's daughters emerged with twisted ideas about sex. In fact, when they did get married, they could no more enjoy or even tolerate sex with their husbands than a dog enjoys getting its teeth brushed or a cat tolerates a bath. They couldn't bear for their husbands to see them naked and went to bed every night in floor-length flannel nightgowns buttoned up to the chin. After a year of this, the husbands were threatening divorce.

What did the daughters do? The obvious! They drugged their father and tried to rape him. You can't blame them. Think of their role models. If the Lord could reward a father for offering his daughters to be raped, and had no quarrel with daughters getting their father drunk and raping him to preserve his seed, perhaps He would look favorably on *these* daughters offering to rape *their* father (perhaps not exactly *offering*, but going ahead and doing it), in order to ... to what? Just because? As I say, their ideas about sex had become twisted. In any case, fortunately or unfortunately, their plan went awry.

They waited until their mother was away at a conference organizing state-wide prayer circles. At dinner they slipped an Oxycontin into one quadrant of the casserole they'd brought and served it up. Dad retired early, apologizing for being so drowsy. Once he was out, they entered the bedroom where he was sleeping, dead to the world, his arms at his sides like a corpse. The plan was to get the johnson stiff, kneel over it—each daughter in turn—and, hiking up their ankle-length dresses, lower the corresponding apertures onto it.

What they hadn't anticipated was that before the consummation could occur, their father would come awake during the procedure.

When they saw one of his eyes flutter open, they panicked. The older daughter was so rattled by his expression that she grabbed up a hand-embroidered "Jesus Loves You" bolster and pressed it against his face to keep from having to see the smile of pleasure (or should I say the leer) that had appeared on his lips. She had been straddling him—the other daughter sitting on his legs—and now they both fell forward in confusion. They mistook his heaving chest, bucking hips, and strained panting for signs of a fully conscious experience of orgasm, which, to an even *greater* degree, grossed them out. Their only thought was to suppress it.

Within a few minutes, the panting and heaving and bucking ended and they dismounted in relief. It took them no time to realize they'd accidentally suffocated him. They both had some acquaintance with CPR and did their best, but to no avail.

After they removed the bolster, straightened the covers, turned out the light, and crept off, there was nothing to suggest he had died from anything other than a heart attack. They took away what remained of the casserole and left the scene for their mother to find when she came home in the morning. She was a competent woman and would know what to do. Without any evidence to rouse suspicions, his death was chalked up to heart failure due to the stress of his suddenly being in command of the country.

Of course the daughters felt sad. And terribly guilty. But in *Numbers* (35:9-34) God forgave *accidental* death and even provided unintentional killers with cities of refuge in case vengeful relatives came after them. In any case, the daughters themselves couldn't be both the killers and the vengeful relatives, so it was all moot. That was a relief.

Still, they felt the urge to confess to someone. Who better than their pastor? They told him the entire story, from its Biblical underpinnings to the accidental smothering. He listened sympathetically and prayed with them. He consoled them by saying that the Lord had called their father home, and chosen them to be the vehicle for taking him there.

He promised to keep their secret. But as a matter of principle, he confided in his wife (they kept nothing from each other) and she told her best friend at church. Inevitably, the story leaked and ended up in the tabloids, but no one wanted to admit that they would read or believe anything printed in *those* rags.

After all these events, the largely ceremonial and powerless President Pro Tem of the other legislative body got nervous and, wondering if the title was worth the risk, resigned. Members of the cabinet, whom tyrant #1 had hand-picked (not for their qualifications, which they didn't have, but for their loyalty to him), also got cold feet and followed suit. In fact, more and more of the politicians of the majority party (even those *without* daughters) quietly retired from politics to be on the safe side and re-entered private life, at the same time becoming significantly more respectful and solicitous of their female children.

The founders of the country had never imagined the need to specify even more successors beyond these. Thus, the hitherto minority party became, by default, the majority party. So. The succession problem was now solved, and we were headed back to normalcy, and, hopefully, a functioning democracy.

Maybe.

There were still a couple of outliers that could potentially cause serious problems.

Unfortunately, a rival for the same political position that tyrant #1 had held (before his demise), was all set to run again. If he won, he would be the most powerful man in the world. He had going for him that his uncle had been president of the country and his father the attorney general, before both were assassinated. (Maybe not such a good omen.)

This guy's distinctive ice-blue eyes did little to offset the chronic voice disorder which gave him a shaky, raspy voice, afflicting his every utterance.

Furthermore, his moral compass was profoundly off kilter. Like his illustrious forebears, he himself was known as a "serial philanderer." His second wife discovered his journal, describing thirty-seven extramarital sexual encounters. The man also sent to friends explicit nude photos of women. Ironically, he banned his daughter from social media, claiming she was posting salacious content on Instagram. In spite of all this, he did have a shot at the highest office in the land.

Back in 2010, he had filed for divorce. Two years later, his wife hanged herself. Their twenty-two-year-old daughter was disgruntled, to say the least. Her fury rankled for fourteen years before she gave in to it.

The father was an outdoorsy guy who loved animals. At nine-years-old, he read about Camelot in *The Once and Future King* (a story widely associated with his entitled extended family). He was riveted by the art of falconry described in the book and soon got his first bird. From that time on, he hunted with falcons all over the world. This gave his daughter an idea. She picked up the hobby, purchasing two birds for herself—a female and a male she called Guinevere and Arthur.

One day, she visited her father at his home. They talked falcons for a while. She said she wanted a picture of him and his birds, and snapped a few. She told him she had bought two falcons and was trying to think of names for them. "I'm considering Guinevere and Arthur," she said. "What do you think?" She had secreted a small digital recorder in her pocket and recorded him trying the names out. He approved.

Several weeks later, when her stepmother was out of town, she came back, having asked her father to look after Guinevere and Arthur while she was away for the weekend.

For three weeks prior to this, she had been training Guinevere and Arthur to peck—when they heard his distinctively hoarse voice saying their names—at his ice-blue eyes in a life-size color photo of his face. (She had enlarged and printed one hundred copies of the photo for training purposes.) In the final week of the birds' lessons, she stuck small balls of hamburger behind the eyes and taught the birds to strike through the paper and get to the hamburger. Falcons, as you may know, are carnivores.

I suppose you can guess what happened next. She brought the birds over to her father's house, hooded, to keep them calm on the trip. "After I'm gone," she told her father, "take them off their tethers and remove the hoods. Keep an eye on them, and if they get agitated, repeat their names slowly several times." With that, she left, and …

Well, I won't spell it out for you.

You may be shocked at the gruesomeness of this act, but consider the fact that the daughter was a movie actor and had spent months rehearsing her role in "Slayed," a 2020 film about a killer Santa abducting women and murdering them at a sewage treatment plant, where the only survivor is tied up in plastic and dumped in the sewage, with a severed arm floating nearby. It's no wonder she'd become a little bent.

Later, she wrote the falcon story as a screenplay under a pseudonym. (All actors are driven to write screenplays.) It wasn't hard to guess at the real author and the real inspiration. But nothing could be proven. I mean, she did have falcons, but falcons are notorious for sometimes spontaneously going rogue. The screenplay was turned into a movie and made her a chunk of change that would keep her in falcons indefinitely.

Good news all around.

Maybe.

• • •

Remember the billionaire? The richest man on the planet? The guy who was among the first on the scene when #2 got killed by his three-year-old?

He was a pretty bad man. He had a policy, in his multimillion dollar businesses, of union busting; he supported voter ID laws to make voting more difficult; he was against public transport; and was an anti-vaxxer during the Covid pandemic. The guy had so much dough he could throw untold quantities of the stuff at his heartless projects. It was like if you gave a seven-year-old unlimited amounts of cash and no constraints on what he could do with it.

With such immense wealth, he had the potential to buy his way into the equivalent of a one-man government and single-handedly reduce the idea of "checks and balances" to a description of his bank records.

Selfish and exhibitionistic, he burdened his children with esoteric names symbolic of only he knew what. Names like HI ʤɪŋks ɚPIɛ. (In defiance, that daughter chose to go by the names "Really?" or "Real?" or just "R?"). He named a son Y-IKES * ð * Vee-Viii. Another, he called "Cyber 'Rho' Radii." A fourth was named "Jasper" after an opaque, multicolored mineral made up of quartz crystals. He chose it because in ancient Egypt red jasper was associated with fertility.

Needless to say, it was impossible for these children to function normally at a public school. They attended an online school he founded, called Black Hole. Of course.

Did I mention that the billionaire had at least twelve children by at least three different women? With that many children, it was almost statistically inevitable that one or more would be gay, non-binary, or transgender. His "son" Jasper turned herself into a girl and became the delicate-looking, gentle young woman she was meant to be.

The billionaire responded with characteristic empathy—"My son Jasper is dead, killed by the woke virus." He belittled her, as a child, for being "queer" and viciously yelled at her for having a voice that was "too high."

When she was old enough to get transition treatment without

parental consent, it became even more obvious that she had made a logical choice. As soon as she was legally able, she gave herself a nice conventional female name, took her mother's last name as well, and after her father's pal, tyrant # 1, was re-elected, moved to Europe.

Her father relocated his headquarters from California to Texas to protest a California law stating that teachers "shall not be required to disclose trans students' expressed gender identity without their consent." He considered the word "cisgender" to be an insult. He committed forty-five million dollars per month to a super PAC that supported the candidacy of tyrant #1 (before #1's daughter ended his life by shooting him in the face).

As you can imagine, the trans daughter had plenty of reasons to feel hurt by, and resentful toward, her father, whom she described as "cold," "quick to anger," "uncaring and narcissistic," "cruel."

A pretty discouraging state of affairs.

Maybe.

Back in 2014, a seventeen-year-old transgender girl in Ohio had deliberately stepped in front of a semi-tractor trailer, leaving behind a suicide note outlining the loneliness and alienation she suffered from her parents' refusal to accept her gender identity. They had denied her request to undergo transition procedures, and put her through Christian conversion "therapy" instead. When she told them she was attracted to boys, they took her out of school and kept her off social media.

The billionaire's daughter had heard of this long-ago tragedy as well as contemporary ones. It was an epidemic. Whether gender dysphoric young people were refused the right to transition treatment, or whether they *did* transition and experienced persecution because of it, they suffered mightily and often saw no way out but suicide.

In her very bones, the billionaire's daughter knew she had to neutralize one source of so much persecution and cruelty. She had an idea.

In any family with twelve children (eleven, actually—one had died in infancy), there was bound to be a prankster among them. This happened to be the transgender daughter's twin brother. The two were very close. He visited her when she went abroad. He commiserated.

She asked him to play a little prank.

"I want Dad to understand what it's like," she said.

"He'll never understand," the brother replied.

"Maybe. But it's worth a try."

In some European countries, such as Denmark, medicines could be ordered online without a doctor's prescription. Denmark also allowed legal gender recognition for transgender people over eighteen without requiring psychiatric diagnoses or medical professional certification.

From the Danish Registry the billionaire's daughter ordered a two-year supply of Estrogen capsules.

If she sent the Estrogen to her brother, could he find a way to substitute it for the contents of their father's supplement capsules? The question was how to sneak it into the pills. The father was quite health conscious and with every meal, he took twice the recommended number of his regular supplements: Red Cap© capsules for focus, energy, and overall mental sharpness; Shilajit© capsules for memory, muscle strength, and sperm count; etc.

No problem, her brother said, and thought it a highly amusing trick to play on their father, not really considering the consequences. (The brother was a prankster, not an especially deep thinker, nor an endocrinologist.)

His sister waited for him to report the results.

Within two weeks, her father was complaining of weight gain, nausea, headaches and memory problems. Worried about his health, he upped his supplement doses.

After a month, the billionaire was experiencing gynomastia (breast swelling and tenderness), erectile dysfunction, mood swings, and lowered sperm count. His voice pitch rose from baritone to alto. Hoping to combat these changes to his health, he added magnesium and vitamin B capsules to his regimen, which his son also surreptitiously swapped out for Estrogen.

In another month, the billionaire had put on seventy-five pounds and developed edema in his ankles. His third wife, a popular television actor, had trouble hiding her distaste for his appearance and eased her way into a separate bedroom with the excuse that his high-pitched snoring kept her awake.

His doctor had become concerned about his blood pressure, fluid retention and potential for blood clots, along with the obesity, and prescribed water pills, blood thinners, Losartan and Amlodipine. Need I mention that these too were in capsule form?

He was frequently getting "fag-shamed" when he was out and about, causing him to retreat more and more into the sanctuary of the $50,000 tiny home in Texas he had built to show he was just a simple guy with simple tastes. He avoided his CosmosZ headquarters nearby.

Soon after that, he died of a massive stroke. Mercifully, he didn't linger long as a paralytic with the need for round-the-clock care.

His daughter and her sibling regretted that they'd overdone the prank a bit, but what was done was done. The brother also regretted interfering with the natural life cycle of Gulf of Mexico game fish. He had made sure all the father's remaining tampered-with supplement capsules were dumped in the Gulf. It's still rumored today that transgender barracuda, tarpons, snappers, and groupers have been found washed up on the beach.

The real story would never have gotten out if the brother hadn't emigrated to Moldova, (which has no extradition treaty with our country) and written a memoir.

Okay. There's nothing more to tell. That's how the daughters saved democracy.

All's well that ends well.

And no maybe about it.

SKIN DEEP

At the Pool

I'M IN THE VANGUARD OF the baby boom generation because I was born in early 1946, which was eleven months after the war in Europe ended, and 9 months after we obliterated the civilian populations of Hiroshima and Nagaski. So the boys came home, and now there's a slew of us. And there's something about us that you may have observed without quite registering it. It's the Mona Lisa smile. Have you seen this smile on the faces of women between the ages of fifty and seventy?

For five hundred years no one has been able to say with certainty why Lisa was giving Leonardo that subtle smile. But I can tell you. Leonardo da Vinci captured, in oil paint, a timeless strategy for smoothing out lip wrinkles and lifting jowl droop.

Five hundred years later, we're still doing it, after all our feminist efforts in the 1970s and '80s. And what about young women today playing peek-a-boo with their breasts like courtesans at the Palace of Versailles? At least we boomers had the decency to just go naked.

Now, many of you might find it impossible to believe that there was a time when teenage girls disliked themselves for being *too* skinny. But some of us grew up in the era of Marilyn Monroe and Jane Mansfield.

When I was a young teenager, I used to go down to the swimming pool and lie around, looking attractive. I had this white bathing suit, and I really looked good in it, except for my neck and my collar bones. And my chest. And my stomach and my calves and my feet. Everything else looked great. But I had a hard time getting comfortable. When I lay on my back, my breasts would kind of disappear across my chest. So I would prop myself up on my elbows. But then I thought that made my neck look too long, so I'd tuck my chin in to camouflage it. That, however, made my collar bones stick out too far, so I would press my shoulders back. In those days I had a hollow stomach, and my hip bones practically jutted through my white bathing suit, so I would press my stomach out to camouflage them.

And my calves were too thin, so I would cross one leg over the other to spread the muscles out. I'd have to remember to keep crossing them back and forth so I wouldn't have one tan calf and one white one. Oh, and my feet never seemed to get tan, so I would press them flat, so the sun would hit them at a better angle.

Well, I had a lot of fun down at the swimming pool, just lying around on the concrete for two or three hours looking attractive.

Remember those days? They're still around.

Hairy

SO. MEN ARE AS OPPRESSED as women by beauty standards, are they? Really?

I have yet to see a commercial that tries to make a man feel inferior to other men because his eyelashes aren't thick enough. Are there ads creating a need in men to buy fake fingernails? I don't see Fruit of the Loom trying to sell men padded crotch enhancers that shape and separate. (But maybe they exist on very discreet websites I wouldn't have been privy to while being bombarded with bras for the "well-endowed woman" television ads.) I haven't heard of female plastic surgeons getting rich by injecting silicone in *men's* private parts.

(Wait, yes, a few men do get such injections, but the practice has been virtually shut down due to the risk of serious complications. It seems that the medical profession cares to protect men's bodily integrity. Women's breasts, on the other hand, are fair game.)

For every man who thinks he's too short, there's a woman who has been persuaded that she's too tall. For every man who wants to be big and muscular, there's a woman required to be thin and dainty. For every man who feels bad about going bald there are twenty women who think their hair is too thick, too thin, too oily, too dry, too curly, too straight, too limp, or the wrong color.

Speaking of which, what about body hair? Where did the idea come from that bald legs and bald armpits are attractive? Hairiness is one of those things, like strength, that get erroneously thrown up to us as belonging exclusively to men.

Hairy women are supposed to be abnormal. That's why millions of women all over the country—all over the *world*—starting at puberty, shave the hair off their bodies because they know if they didn't they'd be abnormal. (Yes, I know European women used to be notorious for having the audacity to go sleeveless with hairy armpits, but global advertising has made that a thing of the past.) Gosh, how terrible would it be to have millions and millions of abnormal women running around with their body hair still attached?

The fact is, virtually all of us women have hair to a greater or lesser degree on our bodies. We've got it around our nipples, in a line going down our bellies, on our forearms, our legs and armpits, in our noses, on our chins and upper lips, on the tops of our fingers … which places (apart from the one place that has been given a multitude of hirsute slang names) are apparently top secret.

And since it's top secret, we figure we must be the only one or in a small, hormonally imbalanced group. So we snip it and pluck it and shave it and burn it off—much to the gratification of the cosmetics industry. Gosh, who knew that the hair grows there naturally? Spread the word.

Not to Worry

THESE KIDS TODAY. We baby boomers never could have imagined using the expression "These kids today ..." But I've been thinking about these kids today, or actually, they're not kids anymore, it's this tattoo generation today. I keep imagining the tattoo generation when they're in their eighties. They're in the hot tub at their assisted living facility soaking their arthritic pains and checking out each other's tattoos:

"Stacey, why did you tattoo a long-handled barbecue fork on your breast?"

"It's a tulip on a stem." Stacey pushes her breasts together. Kaitlin puts on glasses hanging from a string around her neck. Wipes the steam off. Inspects the tattoo.

"Oh. Awesome."

"What about that orange and black tat there on like your upper arm?"

"This one? It's a monarch butterfly."

"Looks like it's, like, hanging on for dear life."

When you're a baby boomer, there comes a time when you go to open the refrigerator door and instead you open the broom closet next to it. And you think, All right. This may be a sign. No need to panic. I just have to start getting my affairs in order. Don't want to burden my family and friends. I should review my living will, go on the waiting list for life care, start getting my house ready for sale.

Then you're drying dishes and you're so distracted by these thoughts that you put a spoon in the fork drawer. That pretty much clinches it. Alzheimer's City, next stop. Or maybe it's a brain tumor. Okay. That's it then. I knew this had to come someday. It was inevitable. I can handle it. I'll stop driving. There are buses. The drivers are friendly. They'll tell me where to get off.

But whenever I have one of these mental glitch panics, I take heart from the fact that they happened when I was young, too. The difference is, when you're young, you turn them into a humorous anecdote to entertain your friends with and everyone has a merry chuckle over it.

For example, I remember once when I was in my thirties, I wanted to go to the Salvation Army Store, but I couldn't find a place to park, so I drove around to the back of a gas station across the street and parked there, knowing I could get towed if the gas station owner noticed my car. But I was in a hurry, so I took the risk, ran across the street, into the store, did a quick perusal of the goods, didn't see anything I liked, ran back across the street, around behind the gas station, jumped into my car and drove out. And as I was driving down the street, passing the front of the gas station, I thought to myself Oh, man, I'd better get that car out of there before they tow it.

If you didn't get the point of that story, or if it took you a moment, don't start in on yourself. My twenty-year-old niece had to think about it for a second or two.

Three Wishes

DO YOU SOMETIMES IMAGINE what you would choose if you were given three wishes to be granted?

For me, #1 would be to have thick, wavy hair. #2 to no longer have bags under my eyes. And #3 to have a flat stomach. If only I had *four* wishes, I could get rid of these frown lines. Or the lines on my upper lip. But ... maybe frown lines *and* lines on the upper lip, and bags under the eyes could come under one category for wish #2, like no wrinkles.

So I could have all that and still have flat stomach for wish #3. But ... oh, I sure wish I could have tight upper arms again. And the backs of my thighs tight. Hmm. Well, *those* two could be subsumed under muscle tone. And actually, a flat stomach could go under muscle tone, too. So I could have all of those under one wish.

Okay, so good muscle tone for #3, including tight upper arms, stomach and backs of thighs. Yeah. That works!

Huh! What am I thinking? I need to wish for a good *back*. #3 should be no back pain. Actually, getting rid of my back pain ought to be #1!

Okay. Start over. Pain-free back #1. Thick, wavy hair #2. And ... aren't wrinkles just a symptom of poor muscle tone? I could throw in wrinkles under muscle tone. So, tight upper arms, stomach, backs of thighs, no bags, no wrinkles for #3. Yeah.

What about world peace, though? If I *had* the three wishes.

Okay, obviously world peace should be #1, and ... an end to environmental degradation. And the elimination of poverty. I mean that's the three wishes right there.

But ... you know ... all three of *those* could be boiled down to one wish, like ... an end to the abuse of power! That *works*! An end to the abuse of power. Peace, environment, poverty—taken care of in one wish.

Which leaves me with two personal wishes left out of three. So. Which ones? Well, of course, getting rid of the back pain, that's a given. But which of the other two? Muscle tone? Or thick, wavy hair?

Thick, wavy hair! No contest.

But it is so *frustrating* to have been given only three wishes!

SELF-IMPROVEMENT

Prescription

NEED HELP AVOIDING THE disgusting political news but can't seem to wean yourself off YouTube?

You don't have to wean yourself off YouTube. Let me help with a prescription.

1. Blur your eyes as you cast them over the captions and images.
2. Un-blur them when you find something like "Golden Retriever Tries to Ignore Cute Tiny Kitten" or "German Shepherd with Depression and Therapy Puppy Go From Strangers to Best Friends."
3. Click on the image.
4. Watch the video.
5. Repeat with more videos, as needed. (E.g. "Cat vs. Deer: Cat Runs After Deer and Deer Gets Annoyed" "1800 lb. Buffalo Is The Biggest Cuddlebug" "Trying to Study With a Cat" "Black Bear Spa Day in Hot Tub")
6. If you tire of cute/feisty/disobedient animals, widen your interests: Try these YouTube offerings:
   a. A young man with a trowel, digging apothecary bottles out of 100-year-old privy pits. ("Digging Out a Sewer Line Leads to a Discovery We'll Never Forget" etc.) To date, the guy has 152 videos of himself deep in the mostly Midwestern doo doo. Sometimes he also unearths doll heads, drinking glasses and broken plates, which adds to the excitement. This makes a nice break from mischievous kittens climbing on sleeping golden retrievers. (You can always go back to them if the mood strikes you.)

b. Bee Gees videos from the 1970s when the guys were at their peak and Barry Gibb was his most swoonworthy. (Highly recommended: "Too Much Heaven" 1978)

c. Virtuoso jazz pianist Beegie Adair (another B.G.!) playing soothing standards (she recorded 35 studio albums with her trio; made appearances on over 100 albums). Still going strong until she checked out at age 84. ("Ain't Misbehavin'" "Our Love Is Here To Stay" "Stella By Starlight" "Misty" "Autumn Leaves" ... Need I say more?)

d. If you're in a mellow mood, and don't mind waiting for the climactic moment, nothing beats glaciers calving.

7. Notice that without your being consciously aware of it, the You-Tube algorithm has now stopped popping up those horrifying political thumbnails it thought you were interested in. Poof. Gone. You can stop blurring your eyes now.

Self-Hypnosis
(A performance piece)

[At center stage, a young man wearing a slightly oversized bow tie, very uncomfortable, self-conscious, shy—signs of extreme stage fright—swallowing frequently, sweaty brow. Tremulous delivery with stiff, awkward gestures.]

I AM REALLY PLEASED AT HOW many of you turned out for my lecture tonight. Of course it is free, but I know some of you came here for more than just a free ride. Sometimes I have trouble renting a hall and getting an audience because, hey, I'm not a big name. No one's ever heard of me, I have no credentials, I have no references. But what does that matter? You're in for a fantastic treat and I can hardly wait to give it to you. Ha Ha. Hey, I'm sorry. I get carried away sometimes, and I know you will too, when you hear how self-hypnosis changed my life, and how it can change yours.

[Adopts a "casual" pose.] You folks are lucky, you know that? I didn't have anyone to teach me these skills. I had to learn everything I know from a book I borrowed from the public library and what I picked up as a child watching reruns of The Ed Sullivan show.

Now I'm going to show you how I used self-hypnosis to rid myself of devastating stage fright.

Would you believe that only two weeks ago I couldn't get up before an audience without breaking out in a cold sweat and fainting dead away? *[Gestures illustratively.]* It's a fact, folks. This same personable, dynamic speaker standing before you was once a bundle of quivering nerves. Brrr. But I tried self-hypnosis on this stubborn problem and, hey, I couldn't believe my success.

How many of you are so afraid of being in front of an audience that you won't even raise your hand when I ask this question? See, you're not alone. My word, no. There are millions of people just like you. Well, here before your very eyes, I'm going to re-create the technique which put me on the way to a career as a performer. This is a simple exercise I use whenever I need to get rid of a bad habit or change my personality totally in one day or stop smoking and lose weight in two weeks. It works for me, it can work for you. [Clears throat.]

Now I'll need absolute quiet please.

[Takes out pocket watch from pants pocket. Holds it in front of eyes and swings it back and forth.]

I am getting sleepy. Very sleepy. My eyes are heavy. I can't keep my eyes open. My eyes are closed and I am very, very sleepy.

[Slides pocket watch back in pocket.]

I will count to three and at the sound of three, I will be completely under my power. One … two … three.

[Eyes are closed.]

[Commanding] Can I hear my voice?

Mmm hmm.

Good. Now just to show me how much in control of myself I really am, I'm going to give myself a post-hypnotic suggestion. Whenever I hear the word "thanks" I will bark like a dog. Do I understand?

Mm hm.

Good. *Thanks.*

Ruff!

Thanks again.

Ruff ruff.

Very good. Now, at the count of three I will open my eyes, but I will still be asleep. One ... two ... three.

[Wakes gradually, stares out, unfocused.]

What do I see before me?

[Wide-eyed, terrified.] An audience.

Am I afraid?

Yes!

Describe to me my bodily sensations.

My hands are sweating. I'm going to throw up.

Very good. Now, I want me to forget about the audience for just a moment. I want me to just think about ... um ... think about my feet.

[Glances at feet.]

Good. Now, audience, as you can see, I haven't completely resolved my little difficulty with stage fright, although I'm very close. Almost there! What I need to do now is to let myself lose—in front of a group of people like yourselves—some of my lingering inhibitions. So let's try an experiment and see if it will loosen me up. I need someone to choose—at random—an object in this room. Any object at all. Just shout it out. ... "Chair?" Thank you.

Ruff!

Good. Now I'm going to give me another hypnotic suggestion and I want me to just relax and take it in. Remember, I cannot make me do anything against my will. Do I understand?

... *[Drowsily.]* Yeah.

All right. When I say "Go for it!" I want me to enter into some sort of interaction with this chair and then go ahead and do whatever feels natural. Ready?

Mm hmm.

Go for it!

[Picks up chair, turns it upside down and mimics driving it, steering with its legs.]

Stop. Very good. Okay. I want me to forget about the chair and concentrate again on my feet. My feet are feeling tingly. They are getting very light. They feel like moving. I can't hold them still. Now I want me to tell my feet to do whatever they feel like doing.

Feet, do whatever you feel like doing.

[Begins to improvise dance steps—tap dance moves—time step, soft shoe.]

Okay, good.

Well, that's it for tonight, folks. Join me next week when you will learn how to sing exactly like Tina Turner in just two hours. Good night and thanks—

Ruff!

—for your attention.

[With bewildered frown, he shuffles off to Buffalo stage left.]

[Scattered and desultory applause.]

MODERN LIFE

Annoying Things

ANNOYING THINGS?

Well, there's **Cling wrap**. Have you ever tried to wrangle cling wrap? It's an intransigent, conscious being. Before you even get started, you slice your fingers on the teeth of the dispenser. The box says: "To avoid injury use cutting edge with care." It says this in two places. And yet no amount of care can protect you from either the cutting edge or the product's schadenfreude. Infuriating. But I've learned of a trick (thank you, Google) that simultaneously metes out punishment on the malignant stuff and renders the cling wrap more compliant. Force the dispenser to endure the icy temperature of your freezer. It's worth it despite the space the box takes up. When I bring it out, the cling wrap has learned its lesson, it's more tractable, almost meek. I rip off a sheet, and back the box goes into the cold.

Then there's **Dental hygiene**. Morning and evening. Circular brushing. Up and down brushing. Flossing. (Don't forget to get under the bridge.) A final go-round with the Proxy-brush. Ten minutes you'll never get back. (*Twenty* minutes since you do it twice a day). So boring that you have to prop a book against the mirror and read during the procedure, holding the pages open with a book claw. This helps, but then you become engrossed in the plot and forget what stage of oral care you've already completed. You end up flossing twice or even three times.

Dentistry: You're having an interminable root canal. Your jaw is aching from being agape for the last hour. Experienced Dental Hygienist, yawning: "Yesterday was such a long day. I'm so tired." Dentist (sympathetically): "Are you going to make it?" Hygienist (doubtfully): "Yeah." Dentist continues to yank, drill, grate, rasp. He finishes a step. Hygienist: "Good job!" He is apparently a Just Finishing Dental School practitioner (I had thought I was getting a staff dentist). Across my face, the two discuss their weekend plans, hinting at juicy gossip about someone: "You know who. I'll tell you later."

The **Elevator.** You live on the sixth floor of a retirement residence consisting of six buildings, all of which are traversed by elevators. You have to take one or another elevator several times a day (walking *up* the stairs threatens your heart, walking *down* them threatens your knees). You accidentally (and routinely) get off the elevator at the wrong floor simply because the door opens. Or, someone with whom you don't want to engage in awkward small talk in a confined space walks toward the elevator ahead of you. To avoid getting on with her (him), you pretend to have suddenly forgotten something and retrace your steps. Or, it being too late to avoid the elevator, once you join him (her), you stare up at the floor numbers in lieu of making eye contact. Or, in order to give the impression you don't feel awkward, you deliberately *don't* stare up at the numbers or fidget but stand perfectly still like someone entranced by an inward thought.

The **Post Office line.** Since the Republican budget cuts and moves to privatize all government services, there's only one postal worker, helping a woman with an enormous pile of envelopes which, for some reason, need to have paper postage typed out, pulled from a machine, and adhered to each envelope. You're just finishing filling out a customs form, so you kindly usher a young couple to go ahead of you. You finish the form. The woman with the envelopes is still at the counter. Finally, she's done and the couple steps up and asks for 200 special gift postcards—are they available? Yes, but the clerk will need to go in the back to get them. She disappears for five minutes. Then an inexplicably interminable wait while, after she returns, she does some weird, lengthy calculating of the cost. Etc.

Smart Phones. You make the mistake of saying, for politeness' sake, "Oh, you have a new grandchild? Do you have pictures?" "Yes, right here on my phone! I just uploaded them this morning." The pictures are eagerly sought. The minutes tick by as she searches, muttering indignant imprecations—"Where did I—?" "Wha—?" "I thought I *labeled*—" "Crap!" "Huh?" "Oh for heaven's sake." "*That's* not—." You stand there growing terminally listless, an extraneous part of the scene. You scream (not aloud), "*Close that #%*!! thing! I'm sorry I ever asked! I was just being polite. Release me!*"

Smart Phones 2. You have a friend with whom you seldom have time to get together, but finally you meet at a restaurant. Every time you bring up a subject, e.g. "I wonder whatever happened to the Bee Gees?" she googles it on her device. Siri is baffled by the question, or google sends her to the wrong sites. For ten minutes, it's "Oh come on!" "Why did *that* happen?" "Did that go *away*?" You want to shout, "It was a *rhetorical* question! Let it go!"

Need I go on? I think not.

Appalled but Not Surprised

DO YOU REMEMBER THOSE old-fashioned aluminum ice cube trays that came with refrigerators in the 'forties and 'fifties? You'd pull the lever up to loosen the ice cubes? Well, anyway, I was thinking about ordering an updated version of one of these online, and I found several; one looked good, made of stainless steel, cost $19.95. But first I scanned the customer reviews, and I came across this one, written by "Appalled but Not Surprised." The review was found helpful by one hundred twenty-nine people. Maybe it will be helpful to you.

Here's what "Appalled But Not Surprised" wrote:

This loathsome abomination broke the first time I pulled the lever. The product description boasts that it's made of *'gleaming stainless steel.'* Oh, it gleams all right. But stainless steel? I think not. And, oops! Don't *I* look foolish with that lever hanging from one hand, the tray from the other, and the dividers on the floor. *'Just like the old days,'* it says. Really? Which old days would those be? The days when itinerant quacks went around selling swamp water? As a little girl, I was filled with pride when my parents let me pull the lever of the ice tray and pop out the ice for our lemonade. It worked so easily a five-year-old could operate it. My parents got good use out of those ice cube trays for fifty years, and I'd still be using them if they hadn't accidentally been sent off to the landfill with the old refrigerator. I resent being deliberately enticed with abhorrent gimcracks that promise to bring back your most cherished memories of yesteryear and then trample on your heart while the corporation laughs all the way to the bank. *'Ha ha! Gotcha, you sentimental sucker.'* And no, forget about those automatic icemakers that foist off on you those measly, pathetic chips that melt as soon as they hit the drink. I had looked forward to making the nice, substantial ice cubes I remembered from childhood. Was that just too much to ask? And now, when I send the despicable contraption back, I'll again have to pay the egregious 'shipping' cost and spend time and gas money getting it to a UPS outlet—a win-win for both companies but insufferable psychological and financial loss for me.

Well. This customer review *was* helpful. It kind of got me thinking about those small, everyday conveniences that we take for granted. You know what I mean? Like … oh, like, for example, not having to cross the Mediterranean, packed into an overloaded inflatable raft, hanging on to babies and elderly parents to keep them from falling overboard. You know? Those little comforts of life? Like not having to stumble, freezing, wet, and terrified onto a beach where armed police greet you with buses and take you to a filthy, crowded detention center until they can ship you back to your country where you'll meet certain death?

It's those simple, old-fashioned conveniences that we've come to expect, like the original aluminum ice tray. "Appalled But Not Surprised" had every right to be outraged.

Phones

I HAVE A LANDLINE phone, but the number is not in the telephone book. Telephone books no longer exist for me to be listed in. Although I have kept my phone book from 2010. For sentimental reasons.

I don't own a cellphone, exactly. I have a Tracfone, what's known as a flip phone. It's got no apps, no camera, no internet. Furthermore there's no point in anyone knowing my Tracfone number since I never switch it on and I don't know how to check messages.

However, this does not mean I don't appreciate the many personal benefits of cellphones, or, as they're called today, "phones." So I have listed the top nine advantages of cellphones. And I would like to share them with you.

Number 1: Cellphones give us valuable opportunities to practice patience and acceptance in the face of frustration. Two years ago I would have thrown that telephone book across the room when I could no longer find a listing for any of the numbers I was looking for. Now, I simply close the book and walk away, calmly and gently murmuring, "You useless piece of crap."

Number 2: These wonderful devices teach us humility. Someone comes up behind me and says in a booming, glad-to-see-ya voice, "Hey! How're you doing?" and I feel that pride of the popular for just the second it takes me to turn around with a big smile for the person, who passes me by, talking on a "phone." That will take you down a peg or two.

Number 3: Cellphones nip arrogance in the bud by another means. An example:

"So my new novel is out. It has elements of a thriller—definitely suspenseful, although the suspense is more of a psychological kind. And there's a bit of romance. But I like to think it's plot- and character-driven without being in any sense a genre novel. Sort of like—Hello? Jane? Hello? Jane, I think your phone is cutting out. Are you there?"

Cut down to size.

Number 4: Another advantage of cellphones is the fascinating intimate conversations they allow you to overhear while sitting on a restroom toilet:

> "He wasn't expecting me to come home in the middle of the day. So I come in, and we always take our shoes off when we come in the house, so I was walking quietly. The shocking part was not just that they were in the act, but that they were—"

Here, she flushed toilet, and I missed what the shocking part was. Another example of advantage number one, acceptance in the face of frustration.

Recently I heard a woman in the cubicle next to mine, shouting on her phone over the restroom ambience while asking the veterinarian to renew her dog's prescription for urinary incontinence medicine. I wondered how her vet was interpreting the thunder of rushing water.

Number 5: Cellphones help you to think twice before hoping for empathy from another person to whom you relate private or traumatic events:

> *John:* "It was the closest I've ever come to dying. I was in Mexico. Standing at the edge of the shore, and this pack of feral dogs jumped out of the beach grass snarling and growling and moving in on me and I really thought—"

(RINGTONE)

> *Martha:* "Sorry, John, gotta take this. Hey, Cleo, you're at the Mall? What are you looking for? Well, why don't you just go online for it?"

John: "—I wasn't going to make it. It was the closest I ever came to death."

Number 6: I'm a much more defensive driver since the advent of cellphones. These days, I edge up to green lights, look both ways, proceed very carefully and especially watch for anyone running their mouth when there's no one else in the car. That's where you want to hang a right and go by a different route.

Number 7: The cellphone teaches you never to throw the first stone. You're at a piano concert, in the middle of a quiet Chopin etude, [RINGTONE] You look around, glaring, sneering, shaking your head in disgust. That's when you realize it's coming from your purse. And by the way, what about the ringtones? Could they be any less like a quiet Chopin etude?

Number 8: It's really a boon to young people, the cellphone. When I was a teenager I had to tie up the family phone to talk to my friends about nothing for two hours. Today you see two young people, apparently strangers to each other, walking from opposite directions, talking on their phones. As they get closer, you realize even though they're not making eye contact, they're talking to each other. And when they're four feet apart, they shut off their phones and continue the conversation about nothing without so much as a gap. They don't ever have to be out of meaningless contact with each other, not for a minute. That's a beautiful thing.

Number 9: It used to be if you saw people walking alone down the street talking into the air, you'd assume they were schizophrenic. Now, you assume they're not schizophrenic.

So, that's it. If you have any questions, give me a call. I'm in the book. Oh. No. There is no book.

Space Captain
(A performance piece)

GOOD MORNING. I'm Space Captain Kasten, your training instructor, and this is your final week of the Earth Explorers Training Program.

How are you doing this morning? Did everyone survive Pollution Endurance classes last week? Everyone! That's a good group.

All right. Let's first open up our auras, tune in our receptors, and begin our study of Earth Communication. You may not believe it, but I've been in like Outer Space a really long time. I've been up there to Earth like seven times, so I really do know what I'm talking about?

Okay, now, with every human being you encounter, you first have to establish if it's a woman or a man. You remember from last month's sex education segment that a woman is an Earth creature with two X chromosomes. A man is an earth creature who's missing part of an X.

Okay. ... What? You want a review of chromosomes? All right. Remember that Earth beings, instead of creating themselves from like conscious will, like we do, are created by these little teeny microscopic worms that stick together in pairs shaped like X's. Can everybody make an X, please? ... Wow, that's really good.

Okay. Now, there was a time when nobody even knew these little worms existed. But even then, men felt their lack because of the things they couldn't do without it. Like growing human beings inside their bodies ... bleeding regularly *without any wounds* ... producing nourishment from their chests ... your basic magical, magical things. So of course they felt inferior, and then when they actually saw these chromosomes under microscopes, explaining it all, well, you can imagine they just lost it completely.

So you need to understand this difference between the sexes so you won't be utterly confused when you're trying to communicate up there … Okay, you're puzzled? Don't worry. I'm going to give you some examples.

All right, here on this picture we have the image and the word "man," m-a-n, man. Remembering that males feel so insecure about their missing worms that they have made this word "man" stand for themselves and … everybody else.

An example? Okay sure. Uh… They'll say, "All men are created equal"… You can certainly see the irony in that one … They take it to such an extreme they even say things like "Man carries his young for nine months." I think that's particularly amusing.

I can see you're really confused now. All right. All right. Let's take another example. Here's a picture of a "Boy." Boy means a male child, young in years, not fully mature as in "Not one boy in my Cub Scout Troop got poison ivy." Let's repeat that together, shall we? Not one boy in my Cub Scout Troop got poison ivy. Oh wow, that sounded great.

On the other hand, this word "girl" is used not only for a female child as in "The girl drove her tricycle around the block," but all adult females as in "I'll have my girl type this up for you." Repeat, please. I'll have my girl type this up for you. Okay.

Your logic is going to make you hesitate to call an adult female a girl. And your survival instincts should keep you from ever calling an adult male a boy, for example, "Ask that boy to put his briefcase down and come here a minute, please" because he will put his briefcase down, he will come over and pluck out your receptors one by one.

Oh yeah … uh … keep your receptors invisible at all times because violence is sometimes a product of this insecurity men have about their worms.

All right. If there are no further questions, class is dismissed. And good luck tomorrow. Launch is at 2800 hours.

ECCENTRICITIES

Little Known Facts about the Elderly

AS A BABY BOOMER, I had no idea getting old would be so dramatic. If you haven't gotten old yet, you won't have a clue as to what's coming up, so I would like to prepare you.

Of course, you probably know about losing hair from head to toe like a dog with mange. You know about forgetting the title of your absolutely most favorite movie. Drooping body parts. All you have to do to get up to date on the conspicuous aspects of aging is read the clichés in Walmart's jokey birthday cards for "seniors." Ha ha ha. Such a riot. But there are some changes that Hallmark never heard of. That I never heard of.

First of all, did you know that when you reach a certain age your pee stops smelling of asparagus? I'll eat asparagus, an hour later I pee, get up from the toilet, sniff the air for that familiar fragrance. In vain. It's missing. We've done an informal survey here at "The Home" and 90% of us elderly people can no longer smell asparagus in our pee. This is a fact.

Here's another one. When you're elderly you can commit crimes with impunity. Not only because no one suspects old fogies of anything that requires running away swiftly, but because you will not leave fingerprints. No fingerprints. Gone. They wear off. Like the noses on ancient Greek statuary. Smooth as a baby's bottom.

And then there are your pits. Think about how meticulous you've always been about your pits. Daily showers, peach-scented deodorants, obsessive sniffing, zealous laundering of shirts after you've worn them only once. A thing of the past for most of us once we reach a certain age. It doesn't matter how much you sweat, your pits do not stink. It's true. It's a while before this fact sinks in and you change your habits.

You just can't believe it. But once you accept it, suddenly you've got a world of free time.

There are other surprises. I won't go into them. I'll let you discover them for yourself when the time comes. But I'll just say that some of them, like the pits and the asparagus and the fingerprints are *pleasant* surprises.

Talking Trash Can Lid

FOR YEARS, I HAVE HAD a chronic pain in the—but maybe that's a rude word. I have had a pain ... in the ... but I can use a euphemism. Let's just say it's a pain in the gluteal zone. And let me tell you, it has been a real pain in the gluteal zone! I've tried everything to get rid of it, even a steroid injection, which, for a couple of precious hours made my gluteal zone feel like it had been to the dentist and had Novocaine.

Anyway, twice a day I lie down on an ice pack and I set a kitchen timer for 20 minutes. And then I daydream, drowse a little bit, and suddenly I think, Oh, surely it's been 20 minutes. Ah! I must have forgotten to start the timer. And exactly as I'm having that thought, the timer goes off.

So the good news is that I *didn't* forget to start the timer. The bad news is that I forgot that I didn't forget to start the timer. And the good news is that my brain still has such an accurate time sense that I instinctively know when 20 minutes has passed. This is the kind of thing that preoccupies us baby boomers. It's because we keep getting things. And I don't mean just getting colds or hangnails.

I got a vitreous detachment. There's this jelly stuff in your eyeball that pulls away and leaves debris floating around in your vision. It sounds disgusting, but it's basically harmless and almost unnoticeable after you get used to it. However, occasionally, when I move my head too fast, a piece of this stuff whizzes by in the opposite direction and I'll snatch at it before I realize it's not a fly, it's a "floater."

Then I got tinnitus. In my case, it's a quiet high-pitched continuous tone. The first time I heard this tone, I thought, "Where is that sound coming from?" I checked my CD player, it was off. My computer, monitor, printer—all off. I went outside to see if there was a train idling on the tracks nearby. Nothing. Finally, I covered both ears to block out the sound and that's when I realized. It was coming from inside my head. My brain was messing with me.

So who knew you could get these strange aberrations? I'll hear someone on the radio talking about Lyme disease or flu. They'll say, "Those at risk of the severest symptoms are young children and the elderly," and I'll think, oh, well at least I don't need to worry about—wait a minute. In old age, my brain and body have started teaming up to play practical jokes on me and then sitting back and watching me freak out.

And now, I have a new brain glitch that I've not been able to find one single reference to, not on Google, not on blogs, medical websites, nowhere. I'm going to describe it to you so if any of you has experienced this, tell me about it. Please.

I call the phenomenon Talking Trash Can Lid.

Talking Trash Can Lid happens to me every couple of months several times a day for a week or two. I have no idea why it comes or why it goes. Here's what it is. Oh, and by the way, I am not making this up.

When I hear an everyday noise—it could be the trash can lid lifting, the floor creaking, my tinkling in the toilet,—I will hear, simultaneously, embedded in that noise, a word or phrase or sentence. I'm not *associating* the noise with the words, I'm actually *hearing* the words *inside* the noises.

So for example, I rustled a piece of paper in my purse and in the sound of the rustling I heard "I'm just sayin'" Or the noise of my desk chair rolling on the floor protector. The words were, "I never got a haircut." Taking my hairbrush out of a basket—"Is this a poor time?" Pulling ice out of the ice tray—"River gambling." Tinkling in the toilet: "Try with Great Britain." A wool sweater sliding on nylon: "Not bad, not bad." Water splashing into the sink. "Your aunt had been arrested." The wooden drying rack wobbling in the dish drainer. "Whaddaya think, Missus?"

I've assumed it's a kind of synesthesia. But what kind? I've searched the internet and found no one else who reports this particular type. So. Talk to me, people. Is there anyone out there who has had this experience?

Let me know.

REFLECTION

Exercise in Retrospection

IF SHE HAD IT TO DO AGAIN she would not spend a weekend in an unheated Oxford dorm room under a blanket in the dead of winter with a homosexual boy who said her legs felt rubbery in tights against his bare skin. And she wouldn't attend a student jazz club and stand without moving for three hours and forty-five minutes until the soles of her feet burned because she wanted to appear so enraptured by the music that no one would guess she was ashamed of being unnoticed in her electric blue, acetate mini-dress.

And, when a young man, almost rid of an accent that marked him as the first in his family to attend university, pronounced on a mild afternoon in May that one did not stroll barefoot in the Queen's Botanical Gardens, she would continue to dangle a sandal from each hand, whether it embarrassed him or not.

If she had it to do again, she would visit the British Museum, but more than once, and not only to look at the mummies.

She would eat Cornish pasty, but just on the first couple of days, and only for lunch.

She wouldn't care particularly that her hair flattened and her bangs separated in the sooty air.

And she would not develop a lame knee when it came time to look for an apartment, nor would she stay holed up in a cheap hotel room until her money ran out or have to be shown by the hotel clerk how to use the classifieds or finally limp off to find a bedsitter with kitchenette and shared bath in the home of a family needing extra rent money and be greeted the next day while struggling to bring in her enormous steamer trunk, with a question delivered in the received tones of Queen Elizabeth by the three-year-old child of the house: "Are you going on holiday?" and find that her knee was suddenly functional.

On second thought, maybe she would do that. She would certainly go to Stonehenge at dawn again on a Sunday, but not with a pimply freshman who had borrowed his parents' Mini for the occasion and could hardly wait until Monday's classes so he could let it slip that he had gone to the country with an American bird two years older who put out in the back seat (even though she didn't).

The second time around she would visit Stonehenge with her angel mother, if her mother had not lost her ability to distinguish a mud puddle from a deep pit in the earth, or a plane ride to England from a trip to hell. So she would probably have to go to Stonehenge alone. This time she would not find a ten-foot peace symbol spray-painted on a twenty-five-hundred-year-old monolith.

She might not stay in London at all if she had it to do again, but would go immediately to the Lake District. She wouldn't hitchhike, though, and be almost abducted by a cockney lorry driver and driven down a dead-end road through a forest, and roughly propositioned and have to jump from the cab and run back down the road to the highway and be rescued by an old woman driving a Bentley with a shawl over her knees, who would scold her for taking risks. This time she would not find a ten-foot peace symbol spray-painted on a twenty-five-hundred-year-old monolith.

And when she got to the Lake District she would ask to stay in an empty castle-turned-youth-hostel just for one night, and she would wake up in the morning shivering and be locked out for the day in a steady, cold, drenching rain, and after trudging for miles along open road, would chance upon a country tea room with a crackling fire in the fireplace and a view through bay windows of small brown ponies dotting the windswept hills.

And she and a fellow traveler—met by chance—would spend the afternoon at one of the chintz-covered tables, warming themselves and growing euphoric on cups and cups of constantly replenished strong tea from a fat china teapot kept hot by a quilted tea cosy, and they would consume basketsful of scones with honey and bowls full of sugar lumps and pitchers full of cream (all free for the price of the first cup), and after a while—dry and warm—they would pull paperback mysteries from their rucksacks, and by the waning afternoon light and the fire's glow, savor the fact that in a good mystery you wouldn't know until the end how everything was going to turn out.

Worst Case Scenarios

SO I WAS EXPECTING TO FEEL crappy for two days after getting my most recent Covid shot. Assumed I'd have a fever, causing all my usual aches and pains to flare up. To say nothing of the horrendously sore arm I would get. Dreading this, I scheduled the injection for a day when I had nothing going on for several days afterward, just in case.

Ace pharmacy had hired (recruited? plucked out of kindergarten?) two "student pharmacists" (that's what their badges called them) to do the deed. They sat at a table side-by-side in their little boy pharmacist white coats, each looking about fifteen years old (the boys, not the coats, the coats were quite spiffy) and seemed nervous about giving the shot. (No more nervous than I, I assure you.)

I sat down by the table. The first student pharmacist had to consult with the other student pharmacist as to procedure. Between the two of them, after a few tries, they managed to attach the payload to the syringe, but the injection hurt like hell, the needle having to be inserted in my arm twice, as something went wrong the first time (when I got home I found there were two little holes in my arm), and the second time hurt even worse than the first time. Nurses who deliver these shots (I've had five or six since 2020, but who's counting?) are so skilled that you barely feel the thing go in.)

The upshot (pardon the pun) was that I had no fever or reaction to the injection(s) except for the extreme arm soreness. So now I was worrying, did my lack of a reaction indicate the vaccine didn't leave the syringe and I'm not protected from the virus? I keep hoping I'll start to feel terrible as an indication that my immune system is activated against it.

(Be careful what you wish for!)

...

My mind has been taking me on negative roller coaster rides like this since at the age of thirteen I read first-hand accounts of Holocaust survivors and read Hiroshima by John Hersey. From that time on, I became a pessimist, obsessed with the negatives of the past and the daunting possibilities of the future.

To wit: I'm looking out my windows at the beautiful white fluffy snow coming down. It reminds me of the song "Over the river and through the woods to Grandmother's house we go. The horse knows the way to carry the sleigh through the white and drifted snow ..."

It called to mind a horse pulling a sleigh full of people on slippery snow and ice and how easily it could slip and break a leg. Which led me to think about the days of horse-drawn carriages when men who liked to take frustrations out on animals would whip and beat tired horses to death to make them keep pulling heavy loads.

Then I thought about animal abuse in general and how all over the world today there are animals suffering at the hands of brutal men.

Suddenly I stopped to wonder how I got on this abysmal train of thought. Oh... yes... it was the beautiful snow coming down outside my window.

Last night I watched a documentary about men who fought in the Korean War. Initially American soldiers froze to death or lost limbs to frostbite because they weren't issued winter clothes. They ran out of ammunition and other supplies and suffered terrible losses.

This morning I'm making my bed, talking aloud as always, as if to someone in the room. (Who?!) I'm irate with General Douglas MacArthur, a big WWII war hero even though he left all those American soldiers in the Philippines while he hightailed it to Australia (famous quote: "I will return." He never did), and because of his "leadership" many of the men died at the hands of the Japanese in the Bataan Death March.

During the Korean War MacArthur lounged in Tokyo (waited on hand and foot by geishas?) "helping" Japan rebuild while he sent the

Americans to fight in Korea in October. He was such an arrogant racist that he couldn't imagine the possibility that N. Korean or Chinese ("Gook") communists could actually defeat American soldiers, who in all likelihood would be home before the weather got cold. Therefore, he failed to issue the winter clothes and spent virtually no time in Korea (a country that suffered terribly at the hands of the Japanese and helped us win the war in the Pacific) to see what was going on, only visiting occasionally for photo ops.

I'm ranting on about MacArthur, swearing a blue streak. Suddenly, I stop making my bed and say (aloud), "Kate, who are you trying to convince? And do you really need to discuss the failings of General MacArthur with nobody at 9:00 am while you're putting sheets on your bed?"

Furthermore, it all happened *seventy years ago*!

CONTACT

A Night at the Fights

[Skating rink music, hawkers selling soft drinks, beer and popcorn.]

ANNOUNCER: Good evening fight fans! We have some thrill-packed events on tap for you tonight here at Whimper Arena, where each fighting pair, plus one solo scrapper, will go three one-minute lightning rounds.

You'll be seeing a couple of familiar faces this evening: Martha Peevish, aka Mart the Snark, who holds the middle weight title in the Lovers' Quarrels No-Holds-Barred Division and her opponent, Wanda Carper, the green young fighter from the Bronx, who came from obscurity only two years ago after being discovered by a promoter during a fight at a restaurant in which she threw a plate of mostaccioli into her boyfriend's briefcase. Since then, her career has skyrocketed, putting her in the number 2 slot for Lovers' Quarrels Middleweight Champ. Mart and Wanda will be fighting as surrogates for each other's actual lovers, who, it should be noted, are unqualified amateurs.

Up next will be Violet Dithering, six years undefeated as Internal Conflict world champion. Violet will be going one-on-one with herself over her indecisiveness about a career, her tendency toward unhealthy perfectionism, and her extreme lack of self-confidence.

Last but by no means least, we have a special event scheduled—one you've all been waiting for. You asked for it and we got it: The Susan B. Anthony Memorial Sexism Debate. Guy Peterson, the infamously misogynistic Los Angeles disc jockey whose radio patter has gone down in the annals of woman hating, will be pitted against Diana Donnadaughter, lesbian feminist, concert pianist, and first woman firefighter with the Detroit fire department.

It's going to be an action-packed evening, folks—thrills, tragedy and suspense. We ask you not to lean against, sit on, or throw food or other objects into the ring. Cheering, clapping and whistling are permitted, but no side-coaching, please.

As I said, each fight will go three 1-minute rounds. Judges will be awarding points in three categories: Dirty, Fair, and Mixed.

In the Dirty category, points will be scored for bickering; sulking; throwing in everything but the kitchen sink; crying for effect; lying; rationalizing; using sarcasm, what-about-ism and obscenities; interrupting; guilt tripping; ridiculing; accusing; screaming; threatening abandonment; slamming heavy books on the floor; and one-upping with big words.

In the Fair category, points will be given for assertiveness; honesty; emotional openness; keeping a sense of humor; putting oneself in the opponent's shoes; listening; taking responsibility (using "I" statements); clarifying; and releasing tension by taking deep breaths.

As surrogates for actual lovers, who will remain anonymous, Carper and The Snark will be fighting in the Dirty category. Dithering will fight Fair, while Donnadaughter and Peterson will be fighting mixed tonight.

And now, while our first contenders are getting ready, let's have a few words with Violet Dithering. She'll be going into a single three-minute round. It'll be interesting to see how much ambivalence she can pack into that 180 seconds.

[Announcer takes microphone to Violet where she sits in the first row, chewing her bottom lip and frowning contemplatively.]

ANNOUNCER: Violet, you've been fighting with yourself for a little over six years now. Do you think you're getting anywhere? Do you see an end to it? Where do you put yourself, say, five years from now?

VIOLET: Well, Stephanie, in a sense I've been fighting with myself my whole life. It's only in the last six years that I've brought my struggles to the ring. I think the training and the discipline have been good for me. Before I went professional, I used to wonder what it was all for, you know, why bother? But now I'm a lot more accepting of myself for fighting as much as I do. I guess it's just in my blood.

ANNOUNCER: When do you think you'll be ready to throw in the towel and retire?

VIOLET: You know, I don't think I'll ever completely quit fighting with myself, Stephanie, but I'll probably cut down a lot as I get older and work through more of my stuff.

ANNOUNCER: What would you say you've worked through so far, Violet?

VIOLET: Oh, I'd say my problem with jealousy. That bout at Madison Square Garden in '73 when I went 32 rounds—that was a turning point for me on the jealousy issue, no question about it.

ANNOUNCER: What will you do when you've gotten too mellow for the ring?

VIOLET: I'll probably go into coaching. I like watching these young fighters come up—struggling with their issues. They seem more open and vulnerable than we ever were at their age.

ANNOUNCER: It's been a pleasure talking with you, Violet. I wish you well, and good luck with your fight tonight.

VIOLET: Thank you, Stephanie.

[*Wearing monogrammed robes, Mart the Snark and Wanda Carper appear at the ring with their trainers and clamber over the ropes. They head toward stools at opposite corners. Mart flips through a thesaurus as she bounces in place. Trainers come over to Mart and Wanda to give instructions in low tones. The fighters listen attentively, nodding, asking questions.*]

ANNOUNCER: And now, fans, it looks like our contenders are ready to start, with Wanda Carper in green trunks and Mart the Snark in red. Here's the bell! And ... they come out fighting.

[*Wanda and Mart jump into the center of the ring.*]

WANDA: Where the hell were you last night? I called three times. You said you were going to stay in to work on your artisanal beer brewing project.

MART: I *was* working on my artisanal beer brewing project. I had to go downstairs to borrow more yeast.

WANDA: *Oh really?* More yeast. I smell an excuse to hang out with your "ever so attractive" neighbor.

MART: Smell what you like. Don't you have better things to do than constantly check up on me? You're becoming insufferable.

WANDA: *Insufferable!* Well, la di da. What about when you "forgot" my graduation—the proudest day of my life—and when you drove my car all the way to Peoria without permission and brought it back with an empty gas tank—

MART: That was *five years ago!*

WANDA: And, said my nephew should be in jail for taking a pack of gum from your wallet—

MART: I was *joking!*

[Bell rings. Fighters return to their corners. Trainers crouch beside them, giving advice.]

ANNOUNCER: [sotto voce] Carper put in some impressive jabs, with two accusations, three guilt trips, and four sarcastic remarks in just one minute. Unless Mart can land some low blows and get in some serious counterpunches, she's going to lose the bout.

[Bell rings.]

Here we go for round two. And … they come out swinging!

MART: Are you so obtuse, you can't tell when I'm joking? And so narcissistic you have to have everyone in your life come to see you pull off a graduation by the skin of your teeth? Where was I going to sit anyway, with all your sycophants taking up your allotted chairs?

WANDA: How dare you—

MART: And what about that unnecessary "innocent overnight trip" with your so-called colleague, who just had to have your moral support at a routine business meeting?

WANDA: That was—

MART: At least I didn't call your hotel room three times, or even once, in a paranoid frenzy of jealousy. What's *wrong* with you?

WANDA: [Starts to cry] How can you—

MART: Oh, *that* old ploy. Go ahead and bawl your eyes out. It's not going to work this time. Pull yourself together or I'm out of here. For good.

WANDA: [Rallying] *You* wouldn't go. Who else would put up with your petty complaints and stinginess, and your—

MART: Just try me.

WANDA: —obsession about food. "I can't eat *those* eggs. They're only cage-free, not pasture-raised." "I wanted the '21-Grain' bread, not the '*Whole* Grain bread."

MART: As opposed to your daily dose of McDonald's fries that you're determined to feed your thighs. Which is bigger, your stomach or your eyes? Hey, that rhymes!

[Bell rings. Fighters return to their corners. Mart's forehead gleams with sweat. The trainer wipes it with a towel. Wanda's trainer whispers in her ear.]

ANNOUNCER: What a turn-around! Well, folks, The Snark really took the gloves off in *this* round. And Wanda's "How *dare* you—"? It's hard to believe a pro like Carper would resort to such a lame comeback. To say nothing of, "How *can* you—" and that tired old chestnut, crying for effect? Didn't get a word in edgewise this round. And in no way matched The Snark's sarcasm in practically every utterance and her right-on-the-nose What Aboutism. That really landed. The barrage of big words: "*obtuse*," "*narcissistic*," "*sycophants*." It'll be interesting to see if Carper holds her own against another of these onslaughts. Round three will be the decider.

[Bell rings. Fighters leap up and meet in the middle.]

WANDA: *Here's* a rhyme for you: You're just a flaming hypocrite, throwing another childish fit!

MART: Ooo. So clever. Did you spend the last five minutes coming up with that? You should have been resting your overheated brain.

WANDA: I'll brain *you*, if you don't shut up.

[Spectators gasp.]

ANNOUNCER [sotto voce]: Whoa. A disqualifying threat of violence! She seems to have stopped trying. But Mart won't like winning by default. She likes to go the distance. ... Wait! Hold on. *Mart just spat at Wanda's feet!* Spitting in disdain is disallowed, for safety reasons. What are the judges going to do with *this*? ... They're conferring. ... One of them is shaking her head. ... They're calling the ref over. ... She nods. ... Removes a handkerchief from her pocket. ... She's extending the handkerchief to Mart! ... Will she take it? Humble herself? ... This is the moment of truth. She either suffers the indignity of bending down to wipe the floor or she's out of the fight. ... She hesitates. ... She takes the handkerchief!! This is momentous! The Snark, willing to debase herself rather than lose a championship. That's the mark of a real pro. She wants an earned win so bad, she's willing to— And the referee holds up a finger for each penalty. One for Carper. One for The Snark. ... Now they're even. ... This is an historic moment for the Lovers' Quarrel Division. ... And the ref calls for the clock to start again.

WANDA: Well, it doesn't surprise me to see you bending so low, and I don't mean just paying homage to the floor. It's kind of what you do. Sniffing after every naïve widow with a huge portfolio.

MART: Are you insane? Where do you get this stuff? From the soaps you watch when you're supposed to be working?

WANDA: I actually *do* work. *Physical* work. I don't sit with my butt fastened to an office chair while my eyes are glued to a monitor screen.

MART: Who says you do?

WANDA: Not me. *You.*

MART: *That's* what you come up with? What the hell are you talking about?

WANDA: Oh, *excuse* me. I didn't mean to insult your sedentary life-style.

MART: Sedentary life style?! You call walking eighteen-hole golf courses all week sedentary? While you take a few turns around a dance floor with some old cruise ship geezer who can barely walk?

WANDA: What are you talking about? You're a CPA.

MART: I'm a golf pro.

[A silence.]

WANDA: Wait a minute. Time out. Isn't the guy you're standing in for a CPA?

MART: No. Where did you get that idea? He's a professional golfer. No wonder I'm getting nowhere in this argument. How am I supposed to frame a coherent rebuttal when everything you say is at cross purposes from—

WANDA: Everything *I* say? Weren't you listening? I *told* you his occupation.

MART: You told me April was his busiest time of year, when he does everyone's taxes.

WANDA: When he goes every year to *Texas*. He's got three golf tournaments there in spring. Get the wax out of your ears.

MART: Get the mush out of your *mouth*. If you didn't mumble like that guy on TikTok—

WANDA: What guy on TikTok?

MART: What do you mean, "What guy?" That *guy.*

WANDA: Yeah, you established that it's a guy.

MART: The mumbling TikTok *prankster*. Were you trying to get me to argue absurdly so I'd lose the—

WANDA: I wouldn't have to *prank* you to get you to argue absurdly.

[Bell rings]

ANNOUNCER: And there's the bell. Final round *over*. Well, folks, this may be a *first*. A fight *within* the fight erupted. A fight *about* the fight— What will the judges do about this *meta*-spat? Is there a precedent? ... It looks like they're pulling out the rule book. ... They're nodding, apparently in agreement. ... Ah! *They're calling a technical!* Well this is an anticlimax. ... The contenders are scowling at each other. There might be *fisticuffs*. ... No. The trainers are pulling them away and the ref is setting up the full length mirror in the center of the ring for Violet Dithering's single 3-minute lightning bout with her Inner Turmoil.

While we're waiting, let's have a word from our sponsor:

COMMERCIAL BREAK

FIGHTCO Vendor:

Here's some advice from FIGHTCO, the makers of quality fight products. Does your lover or spouse leave for work, go to sleep, or simply walk out the door in the middle of a fight, leaving you in a state of intense emotional stress? By the time your lover returns, you may have calmed down, forgotten what the argument was about or be left in a passive-aggressive sulk. That so-and-so may never know how much agony you've been put through unless you can prove it with FIGHTCO'S GUILT TRIPPER—a complete kit of stress provers designed to make your lover take your suffering seriously.

The kit includes this light-weight, comfortable TEAR-COLLEC-TOR, which hooks over your ears like glasses and fits snugly against your cheeks so not a single tear is lost. Deep enough to hold tears from crying spells of up to eight hours duration. Raised marks on the container show quantity of tears shed in milliliters.

The GUILT TRIPPER also includes this HIGH BLOOD PRESSURE REGISTER. Designed for minimal interference during temper tantrums, it wraps easily around your arm, registers your blood pressure at its highest peak, and imprints the reading conspicuously on your skin.

If your lover has not returned within 24 hours, the strain of waiting may be affecting your eating and sleeping habits. The GUILT TRIPPER provides two indicators of dangerous food and sleep deprivation or self-destructive over-indulgence.

Holding onto this blue tab, simply swallow this small pellet called a NUTRIMETER, which measures your hydrochloric acid level within seconds after the pellet hits your stomach. Just pull out the tab and check the color of the tape. Allow me to demonstrate. … A sickly green indicates pre-ulcerous emptiness, while a florid pink warns of digestive system overload.

This SLEEP DETECTOR matches the circles under your eyes against this easy-to-read color chart, which comes in Hispanic, Asian, Black and White skin tones. A conversion table will translate the reading into language your lover will understand, from lethargic and bloated to exhausted and weak.

Order your kit today. For only $24.95 you'll have a set of convincing physiological indicators of the suffering your lover is putting you through. When words fail to express how tragic you feel, don't leave it chance; give yourself the gift of scientific proof. Order before midnight tonight and you'll get this free bonus: FIGHTCO will send out a discreet professional photographer to take pictures of you wandering aimlessly through dark city streets, too upset to care about personal safety.

This offer good for a limited time only. Send check or money order to: THE GUILT TRIPPER, Box 1000, Kansas City Missouri, 64110.

[Bell sounds.]

[Violet climbs into the ring and takes a cleansing breath as she approaches the mirror. She stands and faces it.]

VIOLET *[addressing the mirror]*: How am I today?

VIOLET: Better than yesterday. How am *I* doing?

VIOLET: I'm not sure. Better, I think.

VIOLET: I think? Don't I know?

VIOLET: Yes, *definitely* better.

VIOLET: Good. It's about time I conquered this indecisiveness.

VIOLET: That's true. I guess. On the other hand, this might not be the best time to make demands on myself.

VIOLET: I understand why I'd feel that way after all I've been through, but when am I going to start taking charge, if not now?

VIOLET: Come *on*. I don't think I *do* understand why I'd feel this way.

VIOLET: You're probably right. I'm not you. ... Well, I *am*. But still ...

VIOLET: Can we stick with "I" statements, please?

VIOLET: Sorry. I'm probably right. I'm not *I*.

VIOLET: I'm *right*, I'm *not* I. Well, I *am*, but ... Now I'm getting confused. I'm not *trying* to confuse me, am I?

VIOLET: Of course not. Can we get back to the indecisiveness? What else am I indecisive about?

VIOLET: Oh, I name it! Should I go back to school and get further in debt or get a job to pay off the debts I already have? Should I talk to Mom about her neglect of me as a child or let sleeping dogs lie? Is it enough to give a donation to the Free Lunch Program occasionally instead of volunteering there once a week, or is that a selfish cop out? Would it be better to—

VIOLET: Okay, okay. I get the picture. Why am I so hard on myself?

VIOLET: I *have* to be hard. Otherwise I become completely undisciplined.

VIOLET: I'm exaggerating, as usual. I have *plenty* of self-discipline.

VIOLET: Oh really? Give me one good example.

VIOLET: Am I kidding? What about my dedication to my exercise program?

VIOLET: That's only because I *enjoy* exercise.

VIOLET: Or sticking to my avoidance of sugar.

VIOLET: I do eat *dates*, though.

VIOLET: Dates are *good* for me.

VIOLET: I'm right. I *am* being somewhat hard on myself.

VIOLET: There. See? If *I* were me, I'd start dealing with my perfectionism.

VIOLET: Perfectionism? I'm not a perfectionist. Just the opposite.

VIOLET: How do I figure *that*? What about unraveling my macramé project and starting over *seven times*?

VIOLET: That wasn't perfectionism, that was incompetence.

VIOLET: And it was only a place mat.

VIOLET: Exactly. I couldn't even get a place mat right.

VIOLET: Okay, am I being honest with me? Do I really enjoy macramé?

VIOLET: Well, no. I only took it up to keep my hands busy when I'm in my Treatment–Resistant Anxiety group. I'm always tongue-tied around those people. They're such high-brows.

VIOLET: I *hear* me. Have I thought about joining that Passive-to-Assertive-in-Six-Weeks group? The one at the Y?

VIOLET: Wouldn't I feel shy there, too?

VIOLET: I won't know until I *try*. Okay. Come on. Enough of this. How about we go out and pick up a gallon of rocky road?

VIOLET: [Laughs] What the heck, why not? Ice cream doesn't have *too* much sugar in it, does it?

VIOLET: Good one. I'm *hilarious*.

ANNOUNCER: It seems that Violet isn't in the mood for a knockdown drag out with herself today. This sometimes happens with contenders in the Fair fighting category. The argument often peters out. But The Susan B. Anthony Memorial Sexism Debate will more than make up for it. It's on next. You can bet it won't disappoint. Just to remind our listeners, Diana Donnadaughter is a lesbian-feminist violinist and fire fighter. Guy Peterson is a sexist disc jockey on AM station DREK out of Los Angeles.

[Bell rings. Guy Peterson and Diana Donnadaughter come running through the crowd down opposite aisles. They leap over the ropes into the ring. Peterson punches his palm with his fist, Donnadaughter dances on the balls of her feet. Then they charge into the middle.]

PETERSON: If it isn't Miss *Twinkle*toes! Where've I seen you before? Oh right. At the circus. Weren't you the dancing bear? That's quite a thick pelt you got on your legs. Don't it weigh you down when you're trying to be light on your feet?

DONNADAUGHTER: I'm sorry. Were you talking to me? Your mouth was moving, but nothing was coming out. Just hot air. Were you trying to express yourself in some fashion? It must be so frustrating.

PETERSON: Cute.

DONNADAUGHTER: Yes, you are. Like a little baby pig. Oink.

PETERSON: Haven't you heard? "Male chauvinist pig" was already a cliché by 1980. Where've you been?

DONNADAUGHTER: Oh, Guy, don't you know that the old stand-bys never age? Kind of like *you*. You can still be relied on to act like an insecure teenage boy who gets turned down for a prom date and claims he only asked her as a joke.

PETERSON: Well, it sure would have been a joke if anyone had asked *you*.

DONNADAUGHTER: By "anyone," are you, by chance, referring to a male? That *would* be just "anyone." I was choosier than that, Guy. Did you ever wonder why so many girls danced with each other at the prom? I suppose you thought it was because there weren't enough available males. [*Chuckles.*] Oh, how innocent boys were back then. It's kind of sweet.

PETERSON: Speaking of choosy. Could it be that men happen to prefer women who don't look like stevedores?

DONNADAUGHTER: Gosh, Guy, do you even know what a stevedore is?

PETERSON: I know it's something a woman shouldn't look like.

DONNADAUGHTER: You might want to mosey down to the Port of Los Angeles and get yourself a job as a stevedore. Think what a service that would be to the suffering listeners who have to switch off DREK-AM every time they hear your nasal voice on the airways. Of course, you'd have to be able to actually lift a crate of bananas or Ikea furniture parts. But you could work up to it.

PETERSON: And *you* might want to mosey down to the station and try your luck getting a talk show. Women broke into media gigs a long time ago. Oh wait. You're too ugly even for radio. Oops, I mean "unburdened by beauty standards."

DONNADAUGHTER: Right. We're all aware of the rigorous standards the media has for *male* broadcasters. Balding, aging gnomes with puffy eyes and shirts buttoned up to the chin to hide their hairless chests. Sound like someone you know?

PETERSON: What are you complaining about? Women have practically taken over every news and commentary outlet. Commercial *and* public.

DONNADAUGHTER: Mm hmm. As long as they sign contracts requiring that they wear blouses open practically to the navel, skirts up to their asses, hairdos like blonde Rapunzels and make-up so thick you can't see their actual eyes.

PETERSON: Wah wah wah. It's the twenty-first century, Diana, and you're still whining about imaginary discrimination? Those women *want* to look like that. Whatever happened to a woman's right to choose?

DONNADAUGHTER: You want to go there? "A woman's right to choose?"

[Bell rings]

ANNOUNCER: Well, he left himself wide open for that one. And he hasn't done himself any favors in the matter of courtesy. This bout was billed as a Mixed Rules fight—Dirty and Fair—but I'd say he's thrown a slight preponderance of the dirt. Although there's been plenty of dirt thrown from both sides with only a nod to the rules of Fair fighting, mostly from Donnadaughter, and that nod only paying lip service: "It must be so frustrating" "It's kind of sweet." But Peterson's "unburdened by beauty standards" was a nice save. Well, we'll see if they get onto a more civilized track in the next round.

[Bell rings. Bout resumes.]

DONNADAUGHTER: A woman's right to choose, huh? Allow me to retort, Mr. Peterson.

PETERSON: Oh, here we go. I'm sick of hearing about this.

DONNADAUGHTER: *You're* sick? How sick do you think the women feel, forced to carry dead fetuses to term? How sick do you think those Texas women feel with a 56% rise in maternal deaths after the state's 2021 ban on abortion care?

PETERSON: Gee, do you think those deaths might have had something to do with the Covid epidemic?

DONNADAUGHTER: Interesting that it was only 11% *nationally* during the same time period. And that the maternal death rate is 62% higher in states that have abortion bans and serious restrictions on abortion access than in states that don't.

PETERSON: My, my, aren't we the little numbers geek? Do you spend all your free time memorizing stats from fake news outlets? Get a life.

DONNADAUGHTER: Oh yeah. Fake news outlets—National Center for Health Statistics, Centers for Disease Control and Prevention, Journal of the American Medical Association—

PETERSON: Yada yada yada. I ain't interested. I'm falling asleep here.

DONNADAUGHTER: You want more statistics?

PETERSON: Less.

DONNADAUGHTER: Fewer.

PETERSON: Huh? You're correcting my *grammar*?

DONNADAUGHTER: *Somebody* has to. Since you *ain't* interested. But how about the fact that women, across major race and ethnic groups, are paid 16% less than men.

PETERSON: Another statistic pulled out of your ass.

DONNADAUGHTER: Out of the derriere of the U.S. Department of Labor.

PETERSON: Oh boo hoo. I'm so sorry for those poor women who are taking jobs from men who need them—

DONNADAUGHTER: After the men have left them with children to raise alone. Does that remind you of your last two marriages?

PETERSON: If you mean me escaping those two gold-digging bitches, I can tell you, getting away with the shirt on my back was worth being taken to the cleaners.

DONNADAUGHTER: I wasn't aware that there was that much gold to dig out of a clown who blathers meaningless clichés on a mediocre radio program with lower than zero ratings. And by the way, "*bitches*"? Really?

PETERSON: Oh, good. Here comes the language police. It was just a matter of time. Bitches are technically female dogs. Forgive me for being metaphorical.

DONNADAUGHTER: Gee, I would call you a bastard for that remark, but that would imply there was something wrong with your mother for having you out of wedlock, when your father probably made himself scarce as soon as he knew you were coming. Like father, like son. No, I prefer genderless epithets. Asshole, for example. Everyone has one. In your case the term would be *"flaming* asshole."

[Bell rings.]

ANNOUNCER: Well, folks, they seemed to be out of control this round. Came within a hair's breadth of chest poking. It was billed as a mixed Dirty and Fair debate, but they've thrown away all the rules. And now they've got only one more shot to return to some semblance of civility. Can they do it? Is there any hope that the judges won't simply vacate the debate itself? That would leave a stain on both contenders' reputations. So, here we go. Buckle up.

PETERSON: "Genderless epithets!" Of *course.* Gotta get rid of those genderish words. He, she, man, woman, male, female. Recognizing that two genders exist? Abomination!

DONNADAUGHTER: As usual, you miss the point, Peterson. The abomination is language that makes one gender invisible or reduces it to insignificance. Let me ask you, when you refer to a blonde, a red head or a brunette, are ever you talking about a man? And yet, somehow, those hair colors do exist in males. When you tell a courageous woman she's "ballsy," are you suggesting she could only be brave if she has testicles? And yet, women face the ordeal of childbirth with a song on their lips—

PETERSON: No, they don't. They whine about it constantly.

DONNADAUGHTER: You're right. Maybe not a *song* on their lips but an obscenity for some asshole who got them pregnant against their will.

PETERSON: See? It's always worst-case scenario with you feminazis. Every man is a rapist. Everything related to masculinity is toxic.

DONNADAUGHTER: Could it be a normal reaction to the wholesale substitution of masculine words for words that include human beings? To wit: "The most important achievement of early *man*—"

PETERSON: "To wit"? What are you, Shakespeare?

DONNADAUGHTER: "—achievement of early *man* was the invention of fire." Really? I'm guessing the invention of fire occurred to every early human being after a good lightning storm. Or, how about this: "We'll need a lot of *man*power to stuff envelopes this election." You can bet most of that "man"power will be provided by women. And, "Only *man*kind could think the ability to destroy the planet is a sign of intelligence." Oh wait. Men *do* think that. Women don't.

PETERSON: Right. Women are perfect in every way. Is that how the Taj Mahal got designed, outer space explored, computers invented? All those *women* coming up with those great ideas?

DONNADAUGHTER: All those women beating on the closed doors of labs and think tanks locked against them.

PETERSON: Nobody was telling them not to think.

DONNADAUGHTER: Oh, we got the subtext all right. So *strident*, those women at our doors! Hysterical, shrill, aggressive, bossy, *bitchy*. Remember *that* word? Or the great compliments for the secretaries taking notes: bubbly, sassy, feisty, demure.

PETERSON: "Demure!" Who says "demure" anymore?

DONNADAUGHTER: Good one, Peterson. You found one little word out of a mountain of language to nitpick?

PETERSON: Says the supreme nitpicker. So, you propose what? To abolish every word in the English language that offends your delicate sensibilities?

DONNADAUGHTER: Well, weren't we all better off when "stewardess" became "flight attendant?" So much more descriptive. And I wouldn't mind sending other words to the dustbin of history. "Comedienne," "poetess," "act*ress*," "execu*trix*" for god's sake! "Man-made" could do with some benign neglect. Why not "artificial," "synthetic," "manufactured?" And what about "Woman doctor," "Female engineer?" And I could do without "Man and wife." Would it kill you to say "husband and wife?" Or better yet, "wife and husband"—why does the male term always have to come first? "Boys and girls" "men and women," "king and queen," "Mr. and Mrs." Come *on*.

PETERSON: So you're discounting "ladies and gentlemen," "Mom and Dad."

DONNADAUGHTER: The exceptions that prove the rule.

PETERSON: Let me get this straight. You're advocating censorship?

DONNADAUGHTER: What censorship? The words will still be there. In the dustbin, like "betwixt," and "erelong," to remind us of our quaint, antiquated past.

PETERSON: So the poor sap who uses the wrong word in female company will be skewered as a pig by language police*people* who will be watching every word he/she—oops, she/he—oops, *they* speak. And she/he/they will be stepping on land mines every time he/she/they opens her/his/their mouth. Fantastic. A Utopia!

DONNADAUGHTER: There are worse things than Utopias, Peterson. Don't be a pussy. Grow a pair. Man up!

PETERSON: Say *what*?!

DONNADAUGHTER: Relax, Guy. I'm just messing with you. That's what happens these days, when you're a guy. My advice? Take it like a man.

[Bell rings. Peterson and Donnadaughter continue to stand in the middle, glaring at each other, apparently not satisfied with ending there. Reluctantly, they back off when their trainers pull them away.]

ANNOUNCER: What will the judges do with that baffling finish? Was it a coup by Donnadaughter, or a capitulation? "Grow a pair?" "Man up?" Irony or generosity? The decision has to be unanimous among the judges. One female and two male. And was there enough fair fighting in the bout to offset both contenders' dirty tactics? The bottom line is, who won? Donnadaughter got in a lot of content, but Peterson's mocking comebacks repeatedly compelled her into a defensive position. ... Okay, it appears that the judges have come to a decision. ... Yes ... They're handing it to the ref. ... She's reading it. ... *And it's a win for Peterson!* The crowd is going wild, boos and cheers blending in one thunderous roar. How is Donnadaughter taking it? ... She's making her way to the judge's table. They don't look too comfortable. ... Now she's in their faces. Literally in their faces, close enough to— ... Is she going to get physical? *She's grabbing the female judge by the hair!* Oh my god, this is a bombshell. ... She just ... pulled off the judge's blonde wig and tore open the shirt collar! Revealing ... a conspicuous Adam's apple! The judge was in disguise! It's a panel of three males! Donnadaughter grabs up the trophy and holds it above her head. There's mayhem in the audience. Men turning over chairs to get to the ring. Women holding them back. It's a literal battle of the sexes televised right here at Whimper Arena. Cops are starting to enter from all exits. We have to hope there will be an equal gender representation of the police officers. Now—

[Sound cuts out and screen goes black.]

Appraisal

AN OLD MAN HAS BROUGHT a large glass beer stein to be appraised at an antique show. On camera the appraiser tells the man that the beer stein, in which his mother had always saved bits of string and saved coupons, is worth one to two thousand dollars. The old man staggers back as if someone has given him a shove, and when the antique expert says, "Surprised?" he replies, "Yes," and his voice cracks with emotion.

"Did you have any idea it was worth that much?" the appraiser persists; earlier she has put a price of twenty thousand dollars on a teddy bear.

"No—" the old man squeaks. He seems breathless, close to losing control of his voice. The loose skin on his thin jowls quivers and his eyes shine with tears. He swallows. "No," he tries again, "I didn't—" but the voice comes out reedy and high like the mew of a kitten, and his chest caves so his head juts over it and shakes on his fragile neck.

The camera pulls back just before the man's tears spill into the beer stein, which turns slowly on a rotating stand. As the camera moves off the old man's face, he stoops there, slack-armed, and stares mutely into the glass mug as if looking through a window.

Empathy at Dinnertime

THE TELEPHONE RINGS JUST as she sets her plate on the table. She stops, poised for a moment, thinking she might not answer it. But considering the possibility that her ride might be calling to change plans, she takes the call.

"Hello," she says, an edge to her voice. "Oh yes ... Hi ... Susan, listen, I haven't eaten all day and I've got about five minutes to grab some dinner before I have to rush off to a meeting. Could you— ... Are you crying?"

She listens and waits. She shifts from one foot to the other, rubs her hand back and forth over her hair. "What's the matter?" She grimaces. Her chest heaves with a silent sigh. "Aw ... poor baby. Go ahead and cry."

She looks at her watch and taps her foot. After a moment she asks, "Is it your parents?" Happening to glance over at her plate, she frowns. The cat is making its way across the table on silent paws. She snaps her fingers at it furiously, stamps her foot. The cat looks at her balefully and crouches several inches from the plate, fixing it with a stare.

"I know how they manipulate you," she says. "Of course you feel bad. I would too, those bullies."

She walks with the phone to the table.

"Mm hmm ... mm hmm ... Well, I think you're right about that." She pushes the cat off, sets the phone on the table and sits down.

"Were they up for the weekend?" She begins to cut her chicken. "What did they say?" She takes a bite, moves the phone away from the sound of her moving jaws.

"The first thing after they walk into your place they say *that*? Oh, Susan. Don't let them spoil your pleasure. It's a nice apartment. It's perfect for you. You must expect that they're not going to understand how you live ... Yes, well *you* know that isn't true. And anyway, what's it to them?"

The chicken is dry and tasteless. She looks around for the salt. Of course it's back in the kitchen. "Mm hm ... mm hm ... I would say no! ... Can you hold for just a second?" She runs to the kitchen, grabs the salt shaker and hurries back. "So how did that make you feel?"

"Mm hmm, mm hmm," she commiserates. In the long pause accompanying the monologue at the other end, she gets a chance to eat a few bites. The chicken has gone cold.

"They told you they were ashamed of your divorce? I thought they'd quit harping on that subject months ago ... Well, if they choose to be disgraced by it, that's not *your* doing ... But what about *your* feelings? Do they ever consider your feelings?"

She's extremely thirsty and she's forgotten to pour herself a glass of ice tea from the fridge. This time she carries the phone into the kitchen, opens the refrigerator and removes the tea pitcher.

"Your father has been holding that heart attack business over your head for as long as I've known you." She pours the tea as quietly as possible into a glass. When she returns with the glass, the cat is back on the table, poised to pounce on the dried-out chicken.

"Goddamn it!" she shouts and pushes the cat off again. "Not you. Sorry. It's the cat. She got ... underfoot." She settles in the chair again, slugs down her tea and listens. "Of course you feel guilty. That's what he wants you to feel!"

The lettuce salad lies limp on the plate, drowned in its oily dressing. She stirs at it with irritation. "No, I'm not saying that at all. Of course he loves you, but he still sees you as his little girl who needs protecting, and you're not a little girl anymore ... Susan, you're a grown woman and he has to learn to relate to you as one."

Looking at her watch again she begins to eat the salad doggedly. The garlic dressing makes her thirsty, but she's drunk all the tea in her glass and doesn't have the patience to go back for more.

"Mm hm ... Well, it's true, isn't it? ... No! You aren't responsible for his life. These attacks are— ... He did?" She lowers her fork and sits still for a moment. "Was it bad?" She shakes her head and stares at the plate. "Oh boy ... Did he go to the hospital?" Slowly she cuts another piece of chicken. "How is he now?"

She raises the chicken to her mouth but holds it there, fork in mid-air. "Now listen, Susan. You are not to blame!" She makes an emphatic gesture with the fork and the chicken falls off, dropping to the floor. In one magnificent leap, the cat is on it.

"Your father chooses what things in life to worry about. You can't tip-toe around all your days afraid you're going to step on one of his taboos." The cat is making delicate little growling noises in its throat. She does not attempt to separate it from its prey.

"How's your mother taking it? ... Well, that's something anyway. And what have you been doing since then?" The mantel clock strikes 7:00. She checks her watch and sees that it is two minutes slow.

Picking up what's left of the chicken, she finishes eating it with her fingers. She looks around for a napkin to wipe off her greasy hands, but there is none, so she blots them on the tablecloth. Out in the street a horn honks twice.

"Good. ... Listen, Susan, my ride is here. There's no way I can get out of this meeting. I wish I could. But I should be through around 10:00. If you're still feeling punk and want me to come over, give me a call, okay?" She listens, tapping her foot again and chewing on the inside of her cheek.

"Okay? ... Okay. I think you've been very strong ... Yes. Yes, you have. Keep it up ... All right? ... All right. Talk to you later. ... Sure. ... Okay. ... Talk to you later, okay? ... Okay then, I'll call as soon as I get home. Okay, bye."

She hangs up the phone, not quite slamming it down, and races upstairs to gather notebooks and briefcase. The horn honks again. She hesitates on the landing as she comes galloping downstairs, thinking she would like to go to the bathroom, but decides against it and, picking up her house key as she goes, rushes out the door.

The wide-eyed cat raises its head and stands for a moment with its nose working in and out like the gills of a fish. Then it jumps casually onto the table and proceeds to lick the dinner plate clean.

Coming Out Courtesy of Ma Bell

A YOUNG WOMAN HOLDS UP a telephone book, ruffles the pages and with eyes closed puts her finger randomly on a name. "Marge Rosenthal." She dials the number.

"Mrs. Smith, this is Jen Atkinson. ...You're not Mrs. Smith? Sorry, Ms., then. I'm sorry to call you at home but I didn't think there would be a chance to talk privately at work, and I wanted to tell you how I fee— Jen Atkinson. First, I wanted to tell you that I really do appreciate this promotion, and I certainly don't want to lose the opportunity you're offering me, but on Friday after I accepted, I realized that I could not take this position—uh, just hear me out first, Ms. Smith—even though you're a joy to work for, I cannot be at this job without being open about who I am—Who am I? I am a lesbian. I've been a lesbian for ten years, and I want to be able to talk about my lover as freely as you and the others talk about your spouses, and I'm not going to hide it on the job anymore—Just, just a second—That doesn't mean I'm going to make it some kind of issue any more than it's an issue when you talk about Ralph, but I'm not going to hide it, so I called to say thank you for the promotion. Again, I accept it and I intend to start work on Monday as a completely open person. ... I beg your pardon? ... Oh, I'm sorry. Well, thank you for listening. It was a very good rehearsal for me. Bye bye."

Jen opens the phone book again and chooses another name and number at random.

"Hi Dad, how are you? Good! Huh? Oh, I'm getting over a little cold, that's probably why. Listen, this has gotta be a quickie, I'm just rushing out the door and I know you're busy, but I wanted to tell you how wonderful it was being with the family at the holidays and everybody being so supportive of us—no wait—don't say anything. I don't want you to minimize it. It was very nice. Francine had been so scared to come, you know, with the whole family there—all the cousins and everybody—but she was so glad she did. And the thing that stands out most in my mind, Dad, is when Uncle Charlie started pulling out his fag jokes and then he says, Jen, when are *you* going to get married to some nice young gentleman? With Francine standing there beside me, and you went right over and you said, "Jen is not interested in marrying some nice young gentleman. She and Francine have been lovers for years. That was great, Dad! ... Dad? ... Dad?"

She hangs up. Looks up the number again and redials.

"I think we got cut off. Anyway I just wanted to say I appreciated it and I love you. Bye bye, Dad."

Once again, she closes her eyes and puts her finger on a number.

"Hi Mary, it's me. Wait, don't say anything, I—just wait, Mary. I wanta—What? Who *is* it?! Mary, come on! This is getting ridiculous. For two weeks I call you—you're not home, you're in the shower, you can't talk, you're on your way out the door—and now it's "Who *is* it?" This is silly. Mary, we have been best friends for twenty years. We've talked to each other practically every day. We have shared *everything*—all the stuff with Ed and when John moved out and the problems with our kids. There is nothing we haven't told each other. And now, for two weeks after I tell you this thing about myself, you suddenly do a disappearing act. ... What? 'You don't *know* me!' Oh Mary, I know, it seems that way. It seems like you don't know me, but I haven't changed. I'm the same person I've always been. The only difference is that I feel toward women the way I thought I should feel toward men. That's all, and I understand what you're thinking. It's strange to you and you're probably just full of questions and you don't know how to ask them, and Mary, I would *love* it if you would ask me anything you want to ask. I don't care what it is. Really all I care about is that we keep our communication open, you know? Maybe you're wondering, What do lesbians do together? How does she know she's a lesbian? Does this mean she felt this way about *me* all this time? I mean, it's okay if you're thinking these things, and it's fine to ask me. What do you want to ask, Mary? Do you have some questions? ... You have a *lot* of questions? ... Uh ... sure ... uh ... noon Friday would be fine. ... At the Pizza Hut on Main or—? Yeah ... I know where that is. Uh sure, okay. See you then. Uh wait! How will I recognize you? ... Red top and a denim skirt. Okay. Bye.

Shakes her head. Smiles. To herself: "Reach out and touch someone."

Daniel

"DO YOU KNOW HE DIED?"

"Yes. I read it in our alumni magazine."

"You were his first love."

"He was the best man I've ever known. He was exceptional. When I heard he died I felt—"

"You don't have to tell *me*," she said.

"Yeah. You know more than anyone."

Our eyes were filling with tears. I took out two Kleenexes and put one in her hand.

"What happened? Why did you break up with him?" she asked me in her still heavy Austrian accent. "I told him maybe you were afraid of being intimate."

She came from Vienna—Freud and all that. University educated, famous musician friends, husband a professor, fled Hitler, came to the U.S. knowing no English, just the clothes on their backs, with a small child—Daniel's older sister. "You're a lesbian, I heard. Did you know my sister was a lesbian?"

"Tante Erika?" I had met her when I visited David back then. A tall slender woman with thick hair in a bun. Very kind.

Where had Frieda heard this lesbian thing from? Oh, of course. I'd advertised it myself, as if it were true. My wishful thinking in those strange times. Not actually being a lesbian, I'd had no history, no impulse to be discreet, no assumption that people would gossip about me, or if they did, that there could be any fallout from it. My own mistaken belief that I could turn my heterosexual self into a lesbian for political reasons.

It struck me that this had perhaps led to Daniel's never having looked me up when he was between marriages and in my own home-town to visit his mother. She would have told him.

. . .

I could have said, "Daniel, close your mouth when you're eating, it's gross" in the uninhibited way you'd say that kind of thing to a brother, not tiptoeing around at all or sounding momentous about it—just being spontaneous and upfront. A brother would just open his mouth wider to annoy you, but Daniel would have looked a little surprised, maybe smiled sheepishly, and from then on kept his mouth closed.

And I could have said, "Daniel, here's how I like to be kissed." He had never kissed anyone before me. How was he supposed to know? He would have said, "Like this?" "Yes, perfect." And these problems would have been solved in a moment. Only the young can turn a couple of remediable habits into grounds for irrevocable separation. But who talked these things out back then? And at that age? Amazing that I would leave him rather than have two simple conversations.

That long, gangly boy whose wrists outgrew his sleeves, feet just slightly turned out, emphasizing their size. The old man hush puppies, plaid shirts with clashing plaid Bermuda shorts. Who walked loose-limbed, oblivious to the impression he made. He inspired the affection of the jocks in his dorm as well as the studious boys.

I was too young and too shallow to put together the way he dressed was a symbol of survival, having to do with the fact that his parents had fled Hitler—and come to America with nothing. Frieda and Walter, university educated, working as nurse's aides in a mental hospital. Three young children, two in-laws and her own mother and younger sister to care for. David's clothes came from thrift stores—his mother's young life spent clothing and feeding her family with bargains and coupons and hand-me-downs.

. . .

We're in her tiny two-room apartment in a retirement residence, one I am to move into in due time. On the wall, looking out at us, a large framed studio photograph of him transformed into a distinguished, handsome man.

Someone else had bought his clothes for him and picked out the stylish wire rim glasses. He wore a neatly trimmed beard and that open-hearted smile in the picture. And I wondered how his mother had survived his death.

At some point, the point when I had finally shucked off the misconceptions about myself, he had been in my town visiting his mother, possibly walked along a street that I walked and I could have called him and said, "You were the best man I ever knew. You were the only man I ever had truly delightful sex with. I could love you properly now." Just when I had it sorted out, had learned what love felt like—

Oh it's so simple. You just recognize someone you can respect for integrity and kindness and a lack of self-absorption, and you are drawn to those qualities—excited by them—then you know you love the man himself not just his interest in you. It's so freeing. There's no reason to feel threatened or jealous, because what he thinks of you or anyone else is irrelevant to your love of him.

But David's mother told him I was a lesbian. A liberal-minded mother, who could talk matter-of-factly about these things, probably believed this might be comforting in case he ever thought about that long-ago relationship and felt a pang for having been rejected. It was nothing to do with you, my lovely son, she must have reassured him— the girl had been a closet lesbian. Nothing else could have made her reject your decent, loveable self.

If she hadn't told him that, might he have looked me up?

After the first wife ran off with an old high school beau, leaving him and their children, he got snatched up quickly. There had probably been a very small window of opportunity. And then, at fifty-three, he died.

My Dear Owners

Dear Ramji and Priya,

I am relieved to be once again safe in your hands after being held captive for so many years. I am sure you meant well when you "lent" me to this so-called friend of yours, Kate Kasten. Your nature is to be generous and trusting. Who could have predicted that she would treat me (and *you*) so ill?

At first, she seemed to read me diligently and with interest. She kept me by her bedside and dipped into me every night. Then at page 92 her erratic and unbalanced personality began to reveal itself. She started muttering asininities (she does this all the time, I swear the woman is touched in the head!): "*Vasus? Devas? Are they the same?*" "*Pandavas*—good guys? bad guys?" "These princes, princesses, brothers, heirs—I can't keep them straight!"

She began to actually tear her hair.

Frankly, I was insulted. Granted, I am a complex piece of literature, culturally and spiritually deep. But surely, with persistence, a well-educated English teacher ought to be able to keep track of a few divine and secular lineages. I waited patiently for her to finish me and return me to you. But instead the most appalling thing happened. One day she absentmindedly (hah!) moved me from her bed table to her desk. You should see this disorganized piece of furniture—groaning under stacks of unpaid bills, unanswered letters, half-finished stories (she aspires to be a published novelist—*that* will be the day!).

You can imagine what happened next. I could see what was coming the moment she lay the day's mail on top of me—a bank statement, an urgent plea to renew her lapsed subscription to *Poets and Writers*, and a rejection slip from some pretentious literary journal called *Glimmer Train*. Well, that was the end of sweet daylight for me. The days went by and I was soon buried like an earthquake victim beneath the rubble of her pathetic paperwork.

Years passed. I languished. Week after week, month after month, faintly, I could hear her doing her daily exercises, chatting on the phone, talking to herself, scratching her pen across reams of paper. Occasionally, I would feel a minuscule lightening of the crushing weight on top of me as she forced herself to attend to a bill here and a letter there. Sometimes there was a shifting of the load as she re-prioritized the litter of papers and books. I admit, I gave up hope.

Then one day she began a seven-day rampage that shook the house—cleaning, sorting, tossing things into boxes and trash bags, moving furniture—and suddenly the pile lifted and the light of day streamed down on me for the first time in … what, almost a decade? Oh, how lovely it was! I could breathe. My pages veritably fluttered in anticipation of being read, possibly even finished.

She noticed me then. And she uttered the words I had prayed to hear these many years. "I've *got* to return this book," and had the decency to add, "What must Priya and Ramji think of me for keeping it so long!"

In a few hours the job was done. I was wrapped, stamped and taken to the post office. The trip home via the U.S. Postal Service was—well, let's just say it was mercifully brief compared to what I had previously endured. So, here I am. And at the risk of breaking into tears, I must tell you, my friends, it is good to be home.

Your faithful,
Mahabharata (31st edition © 1990)

Overheard

I WORK ON A COLLEGE CAMPUS. You hear some pretty interesting conversations if you keep your ears open.

The other day I overheard two tenured professors in suits, apparently on their way to class. One said to the other, "He was far more stupid than I think I gave him credit for." A whole new slant on the word "credit."

Two students between classes:
STUDENT 1: "Where'd we get the idea of homework?"
STUDENT 2: Yeah. I don't know. I mean the *Greeks* didn't have the idea of homework."
Was he was referring to the ancient Athenians or the Alpha Delts?

It's these fragments that are so intriguing. The tail ends of conversations like, "...which is how we came up with the idea that some infinities are bigger than other infinities."

These fascinating tidbits are by no means confined to the campus. From separate stalls in the restroom, two voices: "Is today Friday?" "No, it's either Sunday or Monday." It was, in fact, Saturday.

I passed two white thirty-ish women Mall walkers. One says, "And she's white! She's *way* white!" Were they talking about race? Or tanning beds? 'Course maybe that's the same thing.

Another two women Mall walkers: "I don't know how they deal with all that external paraphernalia!" Is she talking about males, or police officers?

I was in line at the post office in December, a man was looking at holiday commemorative stamps in the glass case. A woman with him pointed at a stamp and asked him, "What's that one?" Man: That's the black Christmas. Woman: What Christmas? Man: Black Christmas. And that's the Jewish Christmas. Woman: *Jewish* Christmas? Man: And that's the Muslim Christmas. They don't celebrate Christmas at the same time we do … But don't tell *them* that."

I was walking down the sidewalk, and a man and woman came out of their house headed for their car. Woman, looking down at the grass: "Look at these feathers, Herb!" Herb gets in the car and shuts the door. Woman: "There's a lot of feathers around. Look at all these feathers!" Herb starts up the engine. I'm guessing this might be the beginning of the end for this marriage.

At a tennis court, two men are standing at the net pausing between serves. They are discussing baseball.

And then there's restaurants. You might as well just set up shop at a restaurant if you want to observe humanity at its most mundane.

I was at a table near two couples and their out-of-town guest sitting in a large booth. The man on one end of the booth is telling the others a long story about a chainsaw he broke by trying to cut something too thick. In minute detail he described the three or four extended phone conversations he had with the customer service rep who tried to talk him through breaking the saw down and putting it back together.

"But when I open it up, it'll all fall apart and I won't know where all the screws go. And what about the safety gadget?" Everybody in the middle of the booth is pinned to their seat, but the guy on the opposite end rises and leaves the table mid-sentence to get soup from the buffet. Meanwhile, the talker just keeps talking. When the other guy gets back, the talker reiterates everything he missed.

Then the waiter comes and offers more iced tea. "Yes," says the talker. "I'll be peeing all day, but go ahead."

"And all night" his wife says.

"*Two* times a night," the talker corrects her.

One of the other men says, irrelevantly, "Station wagons are coming back. People are getting over that Sport UTE thing."

Then the three men pull out wallets. The guest loses the fight for the check. The talker says, "If we have an argument about this, you're gonna get smacked right in the kisser."

Regretfully for me, they leave.

Sometimes you overhear something surprisingly metaphysical.

WOMAN 1: I've walked by that house every day for six years and I've never seen a soul go in or out.

WOMAN 2: You may not have seen them, but they do go in and out.

WOMAN 1: Who?

WOMAN 2: The souls.

Revelations

THERE ARE SOME THINGS you kind of wish your mother hadn't decided she could tell you now that you're an adult. Not that I don't appreciate her confidence in me. But still.

For example, I hadn't realized that my father was in the habit of sulking. He didn't sulk around us—my brothers and me—not that I was aware of. But I must not have been paying attention to his sulking with her. Unless he didn't do it then, when we were still at home. It may have been a habit he adopted when we grew up and left. I was too surprised (unnerved?) to ask her. And now it's too late.

Her example was this: Playfully, she had tossed at my father a small, bunched-up ball of aluminum foil from her baked potato while they were attending a banquet for a board of directors he sat on. Just prior to the tossing, he had quietly razzed her about scarfing down every scrap of the potato, including the skin. So, in the spirit of teasing (which *he* started), she tossed the foil at him. How was she to know he would consider it undignified to get foil tossed at him at a formal dinner? But he was pissed. Didn't speak to her for the rest of the dinner and hardly spoke to her all week after that.

Apparently this not-speaking situation happened quite frequently if she did something he took as an affront to his dignity. She would then kind of tiptoe around him and his silence for days until the strain ended with her crying. At that, he would relent. She could tell he was remorseful but was incapable of saying he'd behaved badly or that he was wrong. Instead, he would make it up to her indirectly, with a little gift or a considerate action, but no apology.

It was unsettling to know that my parents had these unpleasant contretemps, and as I say, it made me wonder if such things had always gone on and I was just too young to notice. Even at thirty-something,

I still kind of wanted to think my parents had been the models of maturity I had always thought them.

When I was in my fifties, she shocked me with another fact about my father that I would just as soon not have known. She probably told me because by then she was suffering from dementia and no longer had the built-in censor she'd exercised as a mother dedicated to preventing emotional discomfort in her children.

"Bob and I used to go to strip clubs now and then," she said, out of the blue.

"What? Strip clubs? *Strip* clubs?"

"Yes. Well, he wanted to go, so …" Here she trailed off.

"Dad wanted to go to strip clubs?"

Of course I realize that most men have such things on their minds for much of their sentient lives, but to *act* on it? My staid father? I found it hard to picture him at a strip club. For one thing, Omaha is a small city, where he is known in a lot of circles. What compulsion made him risk running into someone he knew? But then I suppose anyone he would have run into at such a place wouldn't have been likely to pass the information along.

"And you went with him? Wasn't that horribly uncomfortable for you?"

"Yes, it was. I didn't like it. I hated it," she said with a painful grimace, "but I preferred being uncomfortable than letting him go there alone."

Yikes.

This behavior from the man who'd once given my mother a week of silent treatment for tossing tin foil?! What did he think he was doing to *her* dignity by showing up at a strip club, with or without her? The double standard made me feel a little sick. I had always thought of my father as fair-minded and, on principle, anti-sexist.

But then it was my turn to be the bad guy. In the counter-culture seventies and eighties I had decided it was feasible to turn oneself gay if one went about it assiduously. I immersed myself in the lesbian community where I lived, waiting for it to "take." Finally, it did. Sort of. Well, not really, but I got involved with a woman and figured the rest would kick in, given enough time and exposure.

I made the big announcement, assuming my parents would be supportive. They were. They made no objections. They welcomed with kindness and courtesy the woman I was "involved" with. I expected no less. These were my predictably liberal parents.

Needless to say, my new identity, not being hard-wired, went by the wayside. I revealed as much to my mother, who passed the info on to my father. No one commented. I carried on blithely being heterosexual again, and that was that.

Until Mom's dementia-fed matter-of-fact revelation that "Those years when you identified yourself as a lesbian was the hardest period of my life. It was the most horrible thing I had to deal with as a mother. I wondered what I had done wrong. I was devastated." Oh boy.

If my mother had been in her right mind, she might not have burdened me with this particular confession. It had gone against her maternal instincts to ever burden us with anything troubling.

Maybe with some remaining spark of sagacity that day, she thought turn-about was fair play. Hadn't I burdened *her* (unnecessarily) when I was at least in my right mind (if you could call it that)?

But that's ascribing a mean-spiritedness that she didn't have. No, that last daunting admission communicated just what I understood it to communicate: You're a grown-up now. You can handle this, and I, in my decline, need to get it off my chest.

And did I engage *her* from an adult perspective? Did I ask her about her inner life, draw her out on her political ideas, her favorite books, movies, music, her feelings about sex, marriage, motherhood, friendship, death? No. She was treating me as an adult while I remained singularly incurious about her.

Sadly, I've finally grown up. And it's too late.

In The Waiting Room

A YOUNG WOMAN BROUGHT along a book to read while waiting to have her teeth cleaned at the University Dental Clinic. There was always a full waiting room with dozens of people seated on chairs and sofas, spilling over into the hallway.

Determined to put this time to good use, she had chosen a very dry and useful book from which she had been taking notes for weeks. The book was long overdue at the library, but it was much in demand and she was not going to take it back until she finished it. In a few hours she would be attending a meeting where the book would be discussed.

The clinic was not the best place to read a book full of sentences like,

Marx understood this dialectical phenomenon of certain capitalist enterprises embodying anti-capitalist premises while maintaining contradictory relations of power within the sub-structure itself.

She had been reading this sentence over repeatedly when a child, all elbows and knees, squeezed into the narrow space on the sofa next to her. The child at once inclined her spindly body at an angle so that her head and half her shoulders intruded between the woman and the book. She gazed at the print for a moment and said, "What are you reading?"

"It's a book about ... politics," the woman replied, without looking up. She wasn't much of a "kid person."

The child, as if doubting the woman's word, snatched at the cover of the book and looked for herself. She studied the title and, apparently satisfied, sat back.

The woman renewed her attention to the tiresome sentence, uncomfortably aware that the child was staring sidelong at her eyes. After a short time the child asked, "Where are you now?"

The woman pointed to the sentence, and the child looked down at it solemnly.

"In ten seconds I'm going to ask you where you are again," she said, and resumed staring.

For a moment the woman felt panicky and read her sentence with extreme concentration. Suddenly she smiled. She turned to the child and said, "I'm afraid in ten seconds I'll be in exactly the same place."

The child frowned.

"You're supposed to bounce your eyes," she said.

"Bounce them?"

"Like this."

The child put a finger on the print and followed it with her eyes as she jumped her finger across the page from one phrase to the next.

"That's how you read faster," she said.

The woman smiled again. "Yes, but that's if the book is easy to read and interesting."

The child considered this remark.

"Aren't there any pictures in it?"

"I wish there were."

The woman held up the book and leafed through it to show the monotonous pages of unbroken print. Returning it to her lap, she began reading again, determined not to be distracted. The child was quiet for a few minutes. Then she said, "Are you trying to get a good grade?"

"Well ... Sort of."

The child nodded sympathetically and stopped staring but continued to watch the woman out of the corner of her eye. They were both silent for a while and the woman actually read several sentences until she stopped abruptly at a word which was, to her, abhorrent.

It was "mankind." She thought it inexcusable for people to use masculine words when they meant human beings. Whenever she came across such an instance in print, she made the only exception to her policy of not marking in library books. Now she pulled a fountain pen from her pocket and drew a thick circle around the offending word.

The child jerked forward, her eyes brightening with interest.

"What did you do?"

"I circled a word."

"Is it a word that's hard to say?"

The woman thought for a moment and glanced at all the people in the room watching them and listening to their dialogue with idle interest.

"It's a word I disagree with," she replied evasively. "But it's usually not a good idea to write in books."

The girl's eyes narrowed. She scrutinized the word with a shrewd expression. "But this is a very bad word?"

The woman wondered how she would approach the subject. Whether she *should* approach the subject. How old was this child after all? Eight? Ten? Would she have learned to speed read at such a young age? She might be older than she looked. It was perhaps not too early for her to consider the problem of sexist language.

But the girl's mother, carrying an infant on one hip, entered the room and caught the child's eye. In a moment, the girl was off the sofa and out the door.

The woman stared regretfully at the empty doorway for a time before shutting the book with a decisive thud and sitting back to endure the wait, which was, after all, no more tedious than reading a book about dialectical materialism.

A Tina Story

I WANT TO TELL YOU about my niece, Tina. Tina is one of those terribly, terribly bright children who learned to talk and do trigonometry while still in the womb—that sort of thing. Tina has a little sister, Susie. Tina is five. Susie is three.

First I have to give you some background for this Tina story. A friend of the family sent Tina and Susie pairs of pink satin ballet slippers, but the slippers were too small, so little Susie could wear Tina's, but Tina couldn't wear either. Accordingly, the parents sent one pair back and reordered a larger pair for Tina.

Anyway, my mother is on the phone long distance with my brother Frank, and they're talking and Mom hears Susie and Tina squabbling in the background. After a while, Frank turns away from the phone and says, "Girls, if you're going to fight, go upstairs!"

He continues the phone conversation. Mom hears more whining and arguing in the background and after a while Frank turns from the phone again and says, "*Tina*, I *told* you you're going to get your ballet slippers next week!"

So they keep talking and pretty soon the fighting gets louder, and Frank's getting exasperated. He turns to Tina and says, "Tina, do you want to talk on the *phone*?"

"Yes."

She gets on the phone and says, "Susie got ballet slippers and I didn't get mine and she was rude she said ha ha and I don't think that's fair because the ones she got were really mine except they didn't fit—. Hey. Who is this anyway?"

COME-UPPANCE

❋

1634 Belleview

A COUPLE OF YEARS AGO I got tired of being kicked out of apartments, so I decided to buy a house. The most I could borrow was $2000, so the only house I could afford was a little one-story shotgun house built for railroad workers in 1885.

When I first bought it, I had to put in plumbing, wiring, a roof, half a foundation, a bathroom, a kitchen and floors. And that was just the cosmetic work.

The termite damage is so bad that everything shakes when you get up from your easy chair. Every time you set foot in the kitchen, the canisters and plates and pots and pans start vibrating against each other. When the phone rings, the window panes rattle. I've gotten in the habit of tiptoeing through the house. I could easily make my way through a forest now without rustling a leaf.

But I love my house. It has a beautiful view. Belleview runs along the top of a high bluff overlooking a vast old warehouse district stitched together by railroad tracks. You can see Kansas City, Kansas, off in the distance and on the other side are the downtown Kansas City, Missouri skyscrapers. At night the lights are spectacular.

Everybody up on Belleview is poor. There's a vacant lot behind my house where people live out of broken-down cars. These people are very tidy. Each Saturday, they rinse out their clothes in the drinking fountain at the park and hang them from the trees. Then they chop down the weeds that have been growing up all week. They re-arrange the orange crates and bed springs in tasteful little conversation groups. On Saturday nights you can hear them singing harmonious Spanish songs together. Around ten or eleven, the relatives and friends who have homes, head on back and the vacant lot people go to sleep on top of the cars and bed springs.

That's my block—Belleview—on the West Side. Most people who live up here stay because they can't afford to live anywhere else. And they have lots of ties here. This is home.

Well, we've been summoned to a "Community Meeting" next month to let everybody have input on a decision that has already been made by a private developer to put up a twelve-story condominium two blocks down the street. This developer, Mr. Perry, has a fondness for the West Side. He says he came up here and looked around and thought, "I want a view like that!"

He's very committed to the West Side, he says, and hadn't really planned to build a twelve-story condominium. That was just an after-thought. He meant to build a three-story home on stilts so he could take advantage of the view. But when he showed his plan to the architect, why his architect said, "Gosh, wouldn't it be more cost effective to fill in under the stilts?" Well, one thing led to another and, golly, before he knew it Mr. Perry was building a twelve-story condominium. Each unit will go for $150,000 unfinished. You'll remember that my entire house cost $2000 unfinished.

I attended the City Council session where he made his proposal. You'd never guess by looking at me (I don't wear power heels or carry a briefcase) that I'm quite civic-minded.

See, in Kansas City, people like Perry can buy up all our homes by right of eminent domain. All they have to do is get the city to agree that condominiums bring in more taxes than railroad shacks.

Now, I should tell you that my best friend bought a railroad shack next to mine. We wanted to grow old together. We pictured ourselves forty years from now sitting on our respective porches, with shotguns across our laps, glaring at each other and saying, "Stay offa my property." I mean, that's an endearing little vision we have. So we really object to being bought out by land speculators.

But we have a plan. Before the developers start taking over, we're going to get historic landmark status for our block as a genuine turn-of-the-century shanty town. We won't paint our houses. The vacant lot people will make a lot of dough letting tourists take their picture. Every two hours the tourists can watch me and Pat come out and try to start our cars.

We're going to re-name the block Mulberry Lane because of all the mulberry trees that grow here. And when the condo dwellers drive down the block on their way home from work, the little street urchins will demonstrate their favorite street game, "Splat," throwing purple mulberries at the white Mercedes.

We'll strong-arm our proposal into first place on the Community Meeting agenda. And pack the room. And tell no one to bathe for the week prior. Two can play this game.

Zoo

THERE ARE MANY IRRATIONAL things in this world, but there are few as irrational as peoples' attitudes toward animals.

For example, going to the zoo is supposed to be a wholesome family entertainment. Think about that.

Think about lions. Think about a four-hundred-pound, eight-foot lion who is capable of running at fifty miles per hour and climbing trees. Who, in nature, lives intimately with a large family of other lions. Who roams on miles of open land.

At a zoo you'll find this animal alone in a cage maybe three times as long as she is, pacing back and forth perpetually until she dies.

Thousands of human beings pass her cage every day and all they ever say is, "Look at the big lion, Debbie. Isn't she pretty? Don't get too close now!"

Why aren't they screaming, "Get that cat out of there. *Now!*" Why aren't they burning down the zoo administration building?

I had an experience at a zoo once. It was a big zoo where the animals weren't in cages but in areas surrounded by moats.

I was at the gorilla compound on a Sunday afternoon. There was a big crowd at the railing, four and five deep. The children were all pushed to the front so they could see better.

It was feeding time and the gorillas had just had a couple of bushels of lettuce and bananas dumped into their enclosure. An incredibly big gorilla was sitting out at the edge of the moat, delicately peeling a banana and staring blankly at the crowd.

All the people in the crowd were pointing and staring and slinging peanuts at this gorilla, and at one point a man held a child up to see and, in a very loud voice, said, "Look there, Mikey. Look at the funny old gorilla eating a banana."

The gorilla looked over toward the man, put the banana down and, never changing its expression, got up, raised its back on the crowd, and very slowly began to produce an enormous green turd. As this turd emerged from its body, the gorilla reached behind, pulled the turd out the rest of the way, turned back to face the crowd, and solemnly ate the turd as if it were a banana.

The parents were grabbing their children and dragging them away as fast they could, saying, "Come on, kids, let's go see the seals now!"

Within seconds the crowd had disappeared and the gorilla went back to eating its breakfast in peace.

You hear of animals in captivity eating their feces, and now I know why. They do it to disgust people into leaving them alone.

Wreckage

IN THE JULY SUN, a highway patrol officer was directing traffic around an accident that had left two cars terribly entwined in the middle of the highway. Its victims had been carried away by several ambulances, whose retreating sirens could still be heard mewing faintly in the distance.

After first colliding, and before meeting again in their crushing embrace, the cars had spun around and around each other, spraying out a rain of personal belongings like a salad spinner spewing droplets of water. Recently contained inside glove compartments and trunks, under and on top of seats and dashboards, and suspended from mirrors, these belongings were now scattered in a perfectly geometrical mandala of debris encircling the yin and yang mass of mangled steel.

Approaching a diagonal row of traffic cones leading drivers toward the shoulder around the wreck, a driver scowled at the tow truck and patrol car blocking sight of the crash.

"Now what, God damn it?" he swore, slamming his fist on the steering wheel. At intervals during the previous twenty miles, he had struck his steering wheel and cursed at sporadic highway construction. Workers had several times flagged him to a stop to let earthmoving machines lumber across lanes, causing him to yell at his wife, "Why the hell can't they do this shit at night?"

Huddled in the back seat, his son had clutched a small plastic train in one hand and stared straight ahead with wide, frightened eyes, ignoring the grand movements of backhoes unloading dirt on the side of the road. The man's wife, in the front seat, stared ahead without comment, her hands in her lap, shredding a tissue.

"This is your goddamn fault," said the man, facing away from traffic to shout at her profile. "We'd be there by now if you weren't so god-damn disorganized. All I ask is one simple thing from you. Get the kid ready so we can be on time. You can't even do something that simple. Now we're going to be late. For a goddamn funeral. Shit!" And he hit the steering wheel again. "Fuck!"

The woman hugged herself, one hand cupping a swollen elbow, which gave off heat through the long sleeve of her blouse.

When the highway patrol officer, a woman, waved them to the shoulder and with a frown, signaled the man to reduce his speed, the man jammed on his brakes, spraying her shoes with gravel, and muttered, "Bitch."

Then he caught sight of the wreck for the first time. "Fuck!" he said again, but this time with a degree of awe in his voice. "I'll bet you a *bunch* of people got pulped in that one!" His wife heard—with a flicker of relief—that his mood had just shifted.

"Check that out!" he said. One car, so crushed that its doors met each other in the middle, curved around the flattened front end of the other vehicle, fitting into it like a puzzle piece. He rolled down his window and hung an elbow out. Drivers in front and behind had slowed to a crawl, also craning for a view.

"Check that *out!*" he repeated. She had averted her eyes, but now she looked.

She did not experience the horror she expected to feel at the sight. The wreck didn't look like what it was. It seemed to be no more than an ugly, misshapen hunk of scrap metal, nothing that she could picture having sped along a highway carrying passengers. But the sight of the commingled belongings strewn in a perfect circle around the wreck, the intimate belongings of strangers who hadn't had an idea what was about to happen to them, gave her a sensation like that of trying to swallow food while crying—the sensation of choking on grief. Even more, she felt a desolate pity for the objects themselves, their being flung out like that and left exposed.

Inside the ring of debris, a box of Kleenex stood upended, one yellow tissue fluttering from the slit. A dozen long-stemmed white chrysanthemums fanned out on the pavement a few feet from a smashed vase. Two shovels lay crosswise to each other like the last pieces in a game of pickup sticks. There was an empty laundry basket beside them and rolled-up socks. Roadmaps unfolded and lifted partway off the ground in the breeze. A dense, cube-shaped package of disposable diapers sat solidly surrounded by wrenches, a flashlight, and a tire iron. A lavender sippy cup was tipped over in a circle of dribbled juice.

There were high heels, one on its side, the other upright. Sunglasses protruded from a brown case. Six or seven T-shirts of different colors were scattered about like splotches of paint on an artist's palette and several pairs of work pants lay with the legs splayed at various angles as if broken.

A dollar bill was caught on the raised forepaw of a teddy bear. There were half emptied grocery sacks, cans rolled into jumbled piles, one intact bag and one burst bag of potato chips, the chips skittering back and forth. Frozen dinners oozed onto the hot pavement from their torn cardboard boxes and cellophane. Loose playing cards.

And scattered everywhere a constellation of small bright objects, unidentifiable at a distance, some in primary colors—children's Leggos or poker chips or puzzle pieces; others metallic and glinting—coins or pieces of glass.

It seemed to the woman that the objects speckling the highway bobbed up and down on the heat waves shimmering off the asphalt like survivors floating near the vortex of a sinking ship. Gather them up! she cried out inside herself. Someone put them somewhere private! And she looked away, unable to stand the sight.

The line of traffic had come almost to a standstill. Her husband continued to creep along, his eyes darting from the wreck to the car in front of him and back again. As he pulled parallel to the mangled vehicles, he stopped the car for a moment. "Christ!" he said, facing them in a kind of rapture. "Bet the suckers inside that mess got squeezed out like toothpaste."

In one continuous movement, the woman let go of her swollen elbow, undid her seat belt, and slipped out of the car. The man turned when he heard her door open.

"What the hell are you doing?" he yelled, plunging across the passenger seat to try to stop her. The car bucked as it jumped out of gear and stalled. He turned back in confusion to start the engine again, and in those few seconds she wrenched open the back door, released the child's seat belt, and pulled him out.

Moving clumsily, she ran toward the wreckage, the child's legs and feet bumping against her hip as she stumbled forward with him into the circle of debris.

The patrol officer, seeing the woman running with her child into the prohibited area, strode after them, shaking her head, her lips starting to form the words "You *can't* ... " But the woman held the child tightly to her breast and ran around to the other side of the demolished cars to the center of the circle, where she turned and took a stand. Her pursuer stepped around the wreck from the right.

"Ma'am! Ma'am!" the officer called to her. Her uniform was crisp and ironed, even in the July heat, the shirt tucked in neatly. The antenna of the small radio attached to her sleeve bounced against her shoulder as she strode purposefully forward.

Only a few yards behind the officer, the woman's husband stormed around the wreck from the left. "Get in the fucking car or I'll break your *other* arm!" he shouted. He had not seen the officer. She stopped to look at the man, and he, uncertainly, stopped too. She frowned at him and touched the handle of her service revolver.

Stumbling on shards of the broken vase, he kicked them away and stomped on the fan of fallen chrysanthemums, grinding them into the pavement. He glared furiously at the officer, his wife, and his child.

The little boy, burying his face in his mother's neck, dropped the plastic train he had been clutching. The officer reflexively scooped it up and put it in the mother's hand. The mother's voice came out husky and indistinct. She cleared her throat and tried again. "Help us," she said to the uniformed woman. The officer removed her revolver from its holster and pointed it at the man. "Get back in your car," she said. "Now. And keep moving."

PLACE

A Vacation

HER PARENTS HAD A SUMMER home on Nantucket Island but for several years after she took her stand on socialism she disdained going there.

A phrase that cropped up frequently among her circle of friends was "the real world." "People have to live in the real world, you know," they would often remind each other, since most of them had spent a good portion of their young lives in the confines of universities and had been protected from this celebrated real world. It was a source of considerable guilt among them that they had spent so many years and so much of their parents' money learning to write essays on "The Lion Imagery in The Iliad" and other subjects of that ilk.

When at last they had rejected their privileged positions as students or fledgling professionals, they found themselves in a kind of limbo. Aesthetically uncomfortable in the proletarian world and morally bound not to re-enter the world of class privilege, they huddled together in little colonies, creating a mongrel culture which unsuccessfully combined the two.

Nantucket Island was the opposite of the real world. With miles of deserted beach, quaint villages, tanned and fresh-faced people, no crime or pollution, Nantucket remained idyllic in the midst of the real world's disintegration. Things were arranged in such a way as to discourage proletarian and petit bourgeois intrusions. Land was expensive, camping was not permitted, and it cost as much as $400 a month to heat an average-size island home in winter.

She had sworn not to avail herself of the privilege of visiting Nantucket, but one day woke to discover that she was about to drive with her parents to the coast and cursed her lack of self-discipline.

Several times along the way she reminded herself that the revolutionary, Rosa Luxemburg, would never have succumbed to the same temptation (had she had the opportunity). The extravagance of the first class motel rooms en route would have shocked that rebel deeply. For the price of the extra double bed, the television, the hum of temperature control, a good revolutionary could have bought a used mimeograph machine (this was 1976) and several reams of paper. Still, she relished the feel of crisp clean sheets and the thought of tiny soap cakes wrapped like gifts for her morning shower.

The last night out they spent in Falmouth, a genteel New England seaside town smelling of pines and honeysuckle. In the morning they had a leisurely breakfast and caught the Woods Hole ferry at eleven o'clock.

Seagulls soared behind the boat, dropping on currents of air to catch bread thrown by the passengers. People walked the deck arm-in-arm, smiling and pointing out bits of shoreline to one another. She found herself a canvas chair nestled up against the life preservers out of the wind, closed her eyes and let the sun warm her face. Beyond the orange and yellow images under her eyelids floated the insane laughter of the gulls and the sound of waves washing behind the boat.

The first view of Nantucket was a long strip of beach stretching across the horizon. As the boat drew nearer, rambling beach houses came in sight. White picket widow's walks perched on their roofs. Someone was riding a horse along the beach through the shallows left by the ebbing tide. A dog bounded along behind.

Passing through the jetties, the boat steamed around the curve of beach toward the wharf where the gray and white town gleamed on its green hillside, crowned by two church spires, one white and one gold. She left her nest among the life preservers to stand at the rail and watch the town grow nearer and more distinct, the gray-shingled houses and tidy gardens, the sparkling white sailboats bobbing beside the weathered pilings.

Like a frame farmhouse embellished with lacy fretwork, the town was at once Quaker plain and dainty.

Her brother John and sister-in-law Anne were waiting for them at the wharf. They stood by their bicycles, smiling and waving as the big steamer eased into its slot. She had always enjoyed the drama of disembarkations—stepping from a bus, emerging from an airplane after a long trip, that suspenseful moment before seeking the familiar faces and hearing the cries of recognition, the sense of her own importance. And this homecoming brought with it the drama of estranged siblings reunited.

She and her brother hugged each other with affection—big sister and little brother replaced by two adults allowed at last to ignore their differences and embrace. Her mother, father and sister-in-law looked on fondly. The air seemed sparkling clear, the chilly breeze brisk and invigorating. The five clustered on the sidewalk smiling and talking, a little island of consanguinity washed by the gentle stream of people flowing toward the town. She was happy.

Her brother and sister-in-law worked as weaver and seamstress in a high-end shop called The Looms. Anne made appliqued quilts and blouses decorated with fine embroidery. John wove rugs and wall coverings. Their work sold for hundreds—some of it thousands—of dollars as wedding presents and Christmas gifts to the Eastern Seaboard's aristocracy. Anne gardened and John played viola in the local symphony orchestra.

John was eager to show off his milieu. "I want you to meet some good people," he said, and took her on a round of calls. There were Anna the basket maker and Peter the carpenter, cordial and serene in an organic garden, where their lively, naked toddler stained her little fingers with strawberries. And there was Sally, who owned an all-woman landscaping business, and her husband Zach, a banjo player in a local band.

They called on the owners of The Looms, Stephen and Danny, and their friend Jo Starker. She had built two tiny cabins, one for a studio, and lived alone in the moors carving and painting wooden birds. Finally, they met Louise, whom John introduced as "the best meditation teacher in the country."

This community of spiritual artists and artisans living a simple life and working for the pleasure of it welcomed her almost as if she were the new bride of a favored son.

Her brother was proud of her, but he worried about her spiritual life.

"What I'm seeing in you through your letters is negativity," he had written, a year earlier. "This does not mean turn the other cheek. Fight when you have to, but when you don't, then start from a positive base."

She had not replied to that letter or communicated with him since. Now he was coaxing her again with his good life and his accepting, loving friends. She smiled at them all and tried to act natural.

After the visits were finished, they drove out to the house by the ocean. It was a plain house on the outside, built to resemble as closely as possible the eighteenth-century Cape Cod style characteristic of Nantucket. Her parents were devoted to old things. They had collected numerous books on Nantucket history, great historic houses of New England, and biographies of island notables written by their descendants. They were staunch supporters of the Nantucket Conservation Association and Historical Society. They deplored the proliferation of houses on the island. Having snatched up their own four acres of prime ocean view and moorland, they bitterly denounced the developers who were cutting the island into pieces.

As they opened the front door, she was struck by the scent of pine from its raw floorboards and rafters, pine logs in the fireplaces, and pine trees outside the open windows.

Inside, sprays of dried moor flowers sat in baskets on mantels and writing desks. Straw mats covered the rough plank floors. Original paintings and line drawings hung on the walls alongside maps of the island and handwoven hangings.

The two downstairs living rooms were low-ceilinged and cozy.

One held an oak dining table eight feet long with all its leaves in. Illuminated by the light of a small brass chandelier, she, her parents, brother and sister-in-law ate dinner at this table with a view of the ocean across the moor.

Upstairs was a spacious living room almost three fourths the width and breadth of the house and rising two stories to an exposed beam ceiling. A narrow stairway led to a sleeping loft on one end. A tall bookcase stood against the west wall, filled with novels appropriate for idle summer reading. A round game table and a writing desk waited for vacationers to while away an evening. A comfortable sofa and two cane rockers were grouped around a big fireplace, and a cluster of canvas chairs faced the windows looking southeast to the sea.

Her mother had accumulated a collection of unusual shells, stones, and bits of driftwood, which she had distributed about the house in hand-made baskets and pottery bowls. All these objects—paintings, baskets, mirrors, trunks, hangings, in subtle colors and natural textures—made of the house a sensory feast. It was an idealized writer's retreat, she thought, and if she could just put aside the disapproval of her conscience, she might actually get some work done here.

In bed that night, propped up against the pillows and covered by a hand-sewn comforter, she watched the purple sky grow dark and fuse with the black ocean. The lamp light glowed through its green shade, throwing shadows between the sloped ceiling beams. Listening to the wind rattling the windows in their casings, she felt like a character in a gothic novel. In fact, the book *Rebecca* lay open on the covers by her hand. She picked it up and romanced herself to sleep.

The next morning she rose at 5:30, packed her writing materials and lunch, and bicycled six miles into town. Though unaccustomed to physical exertion of any kind, she pedaled vigorously up the hills, amazed to find herself enjoying the pumping of her heart and the aching of her thighs. Instead of getting off and walking at the first sign of fatigue, she allowed herself to feel the pain.

At home she was noted for her sluggishness. Clothed in a frayed brown bathrobe and slippers, she would spend much of her time writing and reading and never setting foot outdoors except to go to meetings or speaking engagements. Her complexion was sallow from so much immobility, and although she was thin to the point of being gaunt, her muscles had become flabby from inertia. Now, racing along on the bicycle, she felt released from whatever mysterious bonds had tied her body to a languor her mind had never shared. Suddenly the two parts of her were one, sailing along together with a sea breeze at their back.

It was 6:30 a.m. when she pedaled past the old Quaker cemetery and into the little town. After flying through open moorland, riding into the village was like entering an enchanted forest. Everything was still except for the chirping of early morning birds and the whirring of her bicycle wheels. She meandered up and down the narrow, shaded lanes, peering through half-open gates into secret gardens. Here and there an ancient wisteria vine covered the weathered shingles of a prim old cottage.

Great summer homes surrounded by impenetrable hedges stood on a rise overlooking the Sound. Walking the bicycle down a steep path between two such houses, she made her way to the beach.

It was still early, not quite 7:00, and the beach was deserted. The tide had ebbed, leaving islands of rippled sand rising from shallow pools. Industrious groups of seagulls were cracking shells left by the receding water. She pushed the bicycle across the sand and up to the point where a stone jetty met the shore, found a boulder jutting at an angle from the beach, and set her basket beside it. Having scooped out a hollow in the sand, she sat down with her back against the rock. She took out a pen and notebook and began to write.

For four hours straight she worked, stopping only twice, once to watch the outgoing morning ferry steam slowly past the jetty and across the horizon, and once to watch three ring-necked geese fly low over the water in perfect formation, honking three solemn notes as they went by.

· · ·

That evening the whole family ate together at the house. Their conversation turned to films, which, like books, was an inexhaustibly satisfying subject to a group so convinced of the correctness of its own aesthetics. In the midst of this conversation, she mentioned a film no one else had seen, a documentary examining the United States' involvement in the Vietnam War. The film had been released a week after the war was finally over. She told them how guilty it had made her feel, how much to blame for never performing any act of anti-war resistance which might have sacrificed her own comfort.

"But what good would it have done?" her brother asked. "You shouldn't feel guilty. You do what you can to improve things, but you can't do everything. There are tragedies taking place all over the world. What about the starving in India and the people in South Africa who die in diamond mines? You have to make choices."

"But this war seemed so directly connected to American apathy and greed," she said. "I paid taxes all those years—money that went right into the production of napalm—it never occurred to me to withhold that money. Or when it did, I just rationalized the thought away."

"What would have happened to you if you had? They would have taken the money from you anyway and fined you. And then you would have been left bankrupt. It would have made it much harder to carry on your other political work."

"Yes, but I would have managed. I live among privileged people with endless resources. I wouldn't have starved or gone homeless. I don't see how I can justify hanging on to that privilege when women in Vietnam gave up their lives fighting what my tax money was doing to their country."

He leaned forward and looked at her with compassion. "Listen, there are lots of ways to improve the world and you have to choose a way that's feasible for you. I create beautiful objects, I live simply and ecologically, I expand my own and other people's consciousness through meditation. These are my choices. You work for change, through a radical movement. You educate people with your speaking and writing. I think those are constructive, feasible ways for you to use your talents. Both of our lives are good lives, not evil. Neither one of us has any reason to feel guilty."

At the end of this speech he leaned his tall frame back against the chair, his curly hair haloed by the chandelier's light. He was the picture of benign self-satisfaction so firm and strong that she felt herself succumbing to it. Like the island itself, his was a warm, tranquil voice saying, "This is what's real—beauty and peace and simplicity—everything else is illusion," but a cynical voice of her own was muttering under its breath, grumbling at her family's unpardonable complacency.

She looked around the room, at the plump cushioned easy chairs, the crackling fire, and thought, How ridiculous I am to carry on an argument of this kind in these surroundings.

She said to her brother, "I suppose you're right, but I do still feel guilty" and changed the subject.

The next few days she spent exploring the island, knapsack on her back loaded with food, suntan oil, pens and notebooks, plastic bags for collecting shells. She strung hiking boots around her waist and tied a wide-brimmed straw hat firmly to her head. She was prepared not only to enjoy this leisure but to put it to good use.

Each day she discovered more beautiful and secluded places. On the fifth day she hiked to the end of a narrow peninsula pounded on one side by ocean surf and washed on the other by the calmer waves of the harbor. The ocean beach was white and stark, broken only by a rotting timber, wrenched from the hull of a foundered ship and half buried in the sand. The harbor beach was strewn with shells and stones and seaweed. Little sand crabs scuttled about, darting nimbly from hole to hole as she walked over their subterranean homes.

Several miles out, the peninsula widened and became marshy. In the midst of this marsh was a rise of land covered by a small, dense wood. It was a peculiar place to find a forest and she was intrigued.

She entered it by way of a narrow, tunnel-like road and found herself in a sunless and silent world. The gnarled trees were covered in vines and creepers. The underbrush was thick with poison ivy and exotic ferns. Nothing stirred. Overhead beyond the canopy of leaves the sun was shining brilliantly on sand and water.

She walked hurriedly on until she came to the end of the track. It opened onto a still lagoon. Peering out at it from just inside the shade of the forest, she felt a lifeless hush hanging over the water. All along the edge were piled the carcasses of dead sea-life—bone-white shells tumbled together and bleached brittle by the sun, skeletal remains of fish. Nothing moved, but thousands of tiny holes in the sand suggested a life just below the surface, as if swarms of creatures had suspended their scuttling movements when they felt her foot on the path. She sensed them poised underground with their hideous outsized claws and protruding eyes, waiting to see what she would do.

All at once she realized how very much alone she felt. And in that moment, the exploring and hiking and basking in nature came crashing into question. For five days she had been wandering alone in paradise. But what was she doing there?

Her brother's friends, the basket makers and weavers and wood carvers, had made her uneasy with their utopian serenity. She didn't quite approve of them. They lacked the dutiful ambivalence of those who regarded no choice, no matter how seemingly personal, as without political implications.

Yet she couldn't picture herself pushing politics on such people. It would have made them embarrassed for her, like non-believers at a pleasant social gathering who find themselves being proselytized by a religious fanatic. She certainly did not feel equal to the task of showing them their political responsibilities. At the same time she was wary of coming too close to their outstretched arms, for fear she might not be able to extricate herself. Marching off to the beaches and winding woodland paths, she had taken refuge in pure nature, but here, too, the perfection seemed to press down on her.

Many times in those five days she had longed for a friend from home to keep her on the right path and remind her of the real world. But now she pictured herself with a friend, floating about the island together as if in a great soap bubble. They would be careful not to float too near anything tangible, for fear the bubble might burst and spill them unceremoniously to the ground.

She stood in the path, desolate at the thought that she needed the world to be ugly.

She turned and hurried back along the road until she came out on the beach again. The sun was straight overhead and oppressively hot. The walk back to the highway seemed endless. By the time she reached it her ankles were sore and her feet raw from walking on sand.

The next day was Memorial Day. Her father suggested they all go into town to watch the parade. She was glad to have something specific to do, that could be shared with others. They were half an hour early, so she sat on the steps of the post office writing cards to friends at home.

She wrote:

Wish you were here to enjoy this place. The beaches are like heaven. There is no rape. Old people pick you up when you're hitchhiking. Even the ticks in the beach grass don't hurt you. I love seagulls. See you soon.

After writing three or four notes in this vein, she stopped to re-read them. They struck her as deceptive. She felt an inexplicable need to be having a good time on this vacation, and she hoped that by the end of the three weeks, if anyone asked how the trip had been, she could exclaim with sincere enthusiasm, "Oh! It was wonderful!" After all, it was ridiculous not to enjoy herself, and the euphoric tone of the postcards ought to be the truth even if it was not.

On the other hand, she thought her friends might be just as glad to receive word of some ambivalence on her part. She pictured them reading the postcards and commenting uneasily to each other, "Well, she sure seems to like it there," behind which remark would lie the ever present fear that one's friends were capable of abandoning their convictions and taking up the easy life if sufficiently tempted.

Was she tempted? Would she want to live on an island set apart in time and space from all the ugliness of the world?

She was saved from the necessity of delving into this question by the sounds of a high school band tuning its instruments. Hurrying to the mailbox outside the post office, she mailed the cards and ran to the corner to watch the parade begin.

Already the island's three elderly VFW members in full dress uniform were marching down the street, their short, shaky steps in rhythm with the drums. As soon as she saw them, her eyes filled with tears. She stared ahead without blinking, hoping the tears would evaporate before they could stream down her cheeks.

Ordinarily she was tolerant of this weakness. She had long ago accepted the fact that her eyes would brim over at the mere mention of a sentimental situation. But this time she determined to fight it. She would not wipe her eyes or blow her nose. She commanded the tears to go away. But the band had struck up a poignant, off-key march, and a little contingent of the Coast Guard in stiff white uniforms was rounding the corner. There was nothing to do but give in to the impulse.

After the Coast Guard, came the town police force and then the volunteer fire department—men of all ages and sizes, looking self-conscious and proud as their relatives along the sidewalk pointed them out and waved. A Dalmatian on a leash trotted along beside them.

The high school band in white and navy blue shuffled into sight. These children of island farmers, fisher- and trades-people were haphazardly uniformed in whatever white tops and navy blue bottoms could be found at home. Boy Scouts came next, followed by Cub Scouts and their den mothers. Bringing up the rear, as always, were the Girl Scouts and Brownies. She noted with bitterness that even the big girls came after the littlest boys. Nevertheless, her tears continued to fall.

When the parade reached the steamboat wharf it stopped and spectators drifted closer to hear speeches delivered by island dignitaries. Not surprisingly, the public address system wasn't working, so everyone but those standing within a few yards of the platform had to guess what was being said. A stiff breeze was whipping the flags and making people's cheeks rosy. Her mother and father were standing a few feet away and she could see that they, too, had red noses and watery eyes.

After the speeches, a choir director appeared and, poising his baton in the air, obtained the attention of a small group of townspeople standing beside her. They were huddled together in an effort to share the three or four shabby hymn books among them. Probably because of their humble appearance, she was entirely unprepared for the sweetness of their voices. They sang a mariner's hymn in harmony so exquisite the skin on the back of her neck prickled:

O savior, whose almighty word
The winds and waves submissive heard,
Who walkest on the foaming deep
And calm amidst the rage didst sleep.
O hear us when we cry to thee
For those in peril on the sea.

The song floated upward on the breeze, evoking images of frail humanity pitted against the vast power of primeval ocean. Once again she was crying and continued to cry until the ceremonies were officially terminated by the firing of three guns over the water. As the last boom died away, she headed for the public restroom to compose her face.

She was disgusted with herself, not only for being grossly sentimental, but for being indiscriminately so. The parade, after all, represented aspects of society she most despised. This beguiling bit of Americana was a microcosm of the country's regressive conservatism. It combined militarism, chauvinism, religiosity and sexism all in one. She despised those marching ranks of self-satisfied males, congratulating themselves on their country's domination of the world and their own domination over the affairs of the island. What could there possibly be in this oppressive display to become sentimental over?

The day following the parade was chilly and overcast and she spent the afternoon trying to write at the Atheneum library. At first when she entered the venerable Greek-style building she was pleased with herself for discovering still another writer's sanctuary. It was the perfect quaint New England library complete with heavy oak tables and a tall clock ticking in the entryway. On the walls were gilt-framed portraits of stern Quakers.

She found an alcove in one corner of the stacks, surrounded on four sides by Crafts, How-To's, and Art Appreciation. In the middle was an unoccupied table and chair which she appropriated by spreading out her notebooks, thesaurus and pens.

She had the alcove entirely to herself all afternoon; even so, she was unable to write a single line. After a while she got up from the table and picked a book on whittling from a shelf. She had often thought of taking up whittling as a hobby, but in glancing through the book realized that she had no interest in wood carvings.

It occurred to her that she might as well be back in the city if she was going to waste time browsing through books which were very likely in the public library at home. She went back to the table and tried once more to write, but nothing came. Finally, she gathered her things and returned to the house, lethargic and depressed. She went to bed and slept through dinner.

Then came a succession of foggy days during which she trudged about from one end of the island to the other, trying to find a corner in which to write. It wasn't that the island lacked corners. They were everywhere. Secluded nests among the dunes, quiet spots along the banks of Long Pond. But no sooner would she settle herself in one of these spots than she would grow restless and distracted. Every moving thing, from the wind rustling her papers to a motor boat crossing the horizon, disturbed her concentration. Soon she would grow irritated, cold and uncomfortable. After waiting it out for half an hour or more, she would gather up her things, pack them away in the knapsack, and trudge back the way she had come.

"It's too chilly to write outdoors today," she would tell herself, thinking to go back to the house and work in front of a cozy fire. But on reaching the house she would be overwhelmed by fatigue and spend the rest of the afternoon in bed.

All these days and evenings she had been avoiding her parents. She left on excursions before they wakened and retired long before they went to sleep. In the late afternoons when loneliness forced her to return home, she found it impossible to be friendly. She didn't want to talk and could not smile or look them in the eye. She felt inexplicably wary, like a criminal expecting at any moment to be exposed. The same wariness came over her at the thought of spending time with her brother and sister-in-law, and she made no effort to see them. She would have liked not to feel this way and in fact had difficulty explaining it to herself.

On one foggy day she decided to walk all the way to Smith Point where ocean and bay met in spectacular turbulence. She thought the grandeur of the setting might stimulate her blocked imagination. She was doggedly determined to produce something.

It was a long walk to the Point. She made her way along the beach with eyes cast down, hoping to find something beautiful or useful washed up on the sand. Her parents, while beachcombing, had twice found handwoven fishing baskets which someone later identified as Portuguese. Considering how material objects had a way of substituting for intangibles, she thought a find of this caliber might help to break up the lump of anxiety that had settled in her chest.

A storm in the night had left the beach strewn with indistinct objects that, from a distance, looked like treasures. On closer inspection, however, they became only the ugly and uninteresting refuse of ships and coastal towns. She picked up a white plastic bottle mistaking it for a giant conch. There was fishing line everywhere, hopelessly tangled and gritty with sand. Here and there lay bits of sodden lumber and oddly shaped light bulbs, pear-like with large filaments miraculously intact. She supposed they were a special type used on boats.

She knelt several times in the sand to examine promising looking shells, but on turning them over found them broken. A long seagull feather, sticking straight out of the sand like a dart, shed parasitic mites on her shirt when she went to put it in her pocket.

She walked on for so long with eyes cast down that when the cries of seagulls startled her into looking up, the vast gray sea and sky made her dizzy and she had to stop for a moment to keep her balance. The gulls were wheeling and soaring over the white waves that clashed against each other off the Point. Three or four people in hip boots were standing knee deep in the foam, fishing.

Patient, solid figures emerging from the spray and fog, they might have been the subjects of an Impressionist water color. They were silent, for the most part, but once or twice she heard the edge of a voice cutting the thick air. Occasionally they would reel in their lines, snap their rods like whips and send the lines flying back, all in one elegantly connected series of movements like cats waking, stretching and settling again.

For several minutes she watched this tableau, dispassionately adding it to the collection of beautiful scenes she had witnessed: a secret forest, an old-fashioned parade, ring-necked geese in flight. Now she had come upon Fishers in Mist. When she got home, she would not need slides to prove to herself it had been a good vacation. She had her mental list.

At the same time, she was annoyed. Not once in all her wandering had she been required to share the beach with anyone until now. She didn't see how she would be able to write with people nearby, it would be pointless even to try. She would just have to find a more isolated spot. Never considering the possibility of going down to the shore and passing the time of day with these people fishing, though she was half numb with loneliness, she plodded on across the peninsula and up the bayside beach, out of the wind and the sound of human voices.

Again she walked with eyes to the ground. Here, shells and oddly-patterned stones were abundant and she didn't want to miss a good one. She walked on and on, bent over and stiff-necked. She began to feel driven, unable to do anything else. It was like a fairy tale in which the hero, in a moment of longing has said, "If only I could walk along a beautiful deserted beach forever, I'd be happy" and an evil magician had granted the wish. It was no longer paradise. The beach had taken the place of her tedious route to work or the too familiar rooms of her small apartment. Wearily she sat down in the sand and leaned back against a driftwood log.

As soon as she stopped moving, a stream of anxieties flooded in. First there was her attitude—her resentment—toward the people fishing. She was painfully reminded of an incident that had taken place several years earlier. She and a friend had been to see an exhibit of photographs. One picture, entitled "Coney Island," was an aerial view showing thousands, perhaps millions, of people packed together on the beach like African captives in the hold of a slave ship.

Her companion had asked, "Why would people want to go to a place like that? I'd rather stay home." She had seized the opportunity to give her companion a lesson in class consciousness.

"Everyone needs to get away from home once in a while," she had replied, severely. "Only a privileged few have a choice in the matter. If Coney Island were all you could afford, that's where you'd spend your holiday."

Leaning back against the log, she closed her eyes and contemplated her hypocrisy. The previous night her mother had asked her to explain her beliefs.

"I'd like to know your views on things," she had said.

Little needles of fear darted in her stomach. "Which views?" she replied evasively.

"Well, your feelings about socialism, for one thing. I guess you think things can't be improved without a revolution?"

She suddenly felt like an actor who hasn't learned her lines and is standing alone on stage with the curtain rising. There had been a time when she knew the lines backward and forward and had regularly flung them in her parents' faces. Lately it had been harder and harder for them to drag an opinion out of her.

"I don't like to be pinned down on my political position," she said, "because it makes me feel as if I were expected to have a concrete solution to the problems of the world. And I don't have a solution." Her mother nodded sympathetically as if to say of course you don't and shouldn't be expected to.

She had burned a great many bridges when she had known exactly what was wrong with society and what to do about it. Now, having become not only uncertain, but having experienced something like reversal in many of her views, she was unable to say a word on the subject without feeling ridiculous.

For the five years prior to this she had pursued a life she had thought of as politically committed. It meant attending meetings three or four nights a week, speaking at schools and rallies, writing polemical tracts. This style of living seemed exciting and important and right. "The personal is political" was a slogan not original with her, but one to which she adhered unwaveringly.

The crisis came when she found herself avoiding meetings and wanting to write novels instead. It was very hard for someone who had no habit of moderation to fix on a moderate course. For her it came down to writing for her own pleasure or working selflessly for the movement. No in-between. Of course her principles could be reflected in fiction, but she could not pretend that they would shine through with the radiance her political conscience demanded. They would be subtle and very often compromised for Art.

She was now in the humiliating situation of softening her position, not because she had learned tolerance or moderation, but because she wanted something for herself. And here was a parent asking her to declare what she believed in.

To punish her mother, she slouched into her default morose and nihilistic posture. She said (in rhetoric only a little less thick than this): "The forces of oppression have a stranglehold on the world that's too strong to wrest loose. I can only feel hopeless about working for change and might just as well write novels." (This last spoken with a virtual curl of the lip as if novel-writing were on a par with gossiping at the bridge table.)

She had found there was no better way to put her mother at a disadvantage than to be despondent. It made her mother feel vaguely guilty and compelled to provide a bright side to look on. She was deeply ashamed to find herself using this knowledge against her mother just to save face (better to present herself as a tired, cynical worker in a noble but lost cause, than admit to having become self-interested). She chose to ignore the fact that her mother had lived at least thirty years longer than she had and was probably not deceived.

The parent-child struggle lent an unwelcome lack of dignity to the larger question that plagued her, namely, what *did* she believe in? Once, several months earlier, she had taken out a pen and paper and tried to write the problem out logically, beginning with what she called the Primary Assumption, which was: Every action or inaction has political significance. With this as a condition, she listed three basic necessities in life: 1. To be morally responsible, 2. To become all one could be, 3. To find at least *some* joy in work.

At the time she wrote out these thoughts, she experienced the three necessities as one. She was caught up in a whirl of activity. Working to improve the world was both a vocation and a passion. Then the whirl began to turn more slowly and as it slowed, her needs separated out as in a centrifuge, by weight and buoyancy. There were #2 and #3 floating to the top and #1 sinking, heavy and brooding, to the bottom.

Over her head hung the Primary Assumption like the Golden Rule, only more ominous for having elevated all actions to the plane of worldwide significance.

She was getting cold sitting in the sand, so she rose and continued on down the shore, no longer interested in beachcombing but just wandering aimlessly. A party of sandpipers bustled along in front, stopping at intervals to face her and deliver indignant peeps. They were peeping at her to get her great flapping feet off their territory and to send someone else's prey burrowing out of reach. She stopped to study them for a moment and concluded that they were the most self-important birds she'd ever seen. Abruptly, she climbed over the dunes and pushed across the moor toward home, wondering when this vacation would ever end.

As it turned out, the next few days were not as bad as she had expected. Feeling more sociable, she joined her parents on an excursion to the village of Siasconset.

Siasconset was a little cluster of seventeenth and eighteenth century cottages, huddled together along a bluff, picturesquely named Tom Nevers Head. Narrow cobbled lanes wound in and out among the houses, which leaned crookedly against each other. They were humble dwellings, homes and shops of early fisher-people, carpenters, and rope-makers. Over the centuries these cottages had gained so many additions—bedrooms, pantries, and sheds—that they gave the impression of having reached out to each other in order to draw closer together.

By contrast, a long row of widely spaced summer homes sat along the cliff from the village to the lighthouse, surrounded by velvet lawns and separated from each other by high hedges.

The cliff was almost a sheer drop to the beach. It was covered with a tangle of scrubby pine, poison ivy, and wild rose climbing up and over the steep cliff walls. Down below, the waves rolled in along the beach one after another, inexorable and slow. Beyond the breakers lay the open sea, enormous and glittering in the afternoon sun.

Her mother had discovered a public footpath that wound its way along the cliff edge for about three quarters of a mile. Cutting right across private lawns and gardens, it gave not only a spectacular view of the ocean, but even more exciting, a forbidden intimacy with the great homes.

Most of them were closed, the season being a week off. Porches were bare of the wicker divans and rockers, the potted ferns that suggest habitation in such places. Curtains were drawn, shutters nailed shut and flag poles bare.

The path was narrow and they had to walk single file. From the start her father was uncomfortable. He kept making excuses to turn back: It was late, guests were coming, they'd seen enough and the path might go on for miles. The truth was, he didn't like treading on the front lawns of wealthy people, even though in this case he had the legal right to do so. By municipal law, the owners themselves had had arches cut through the hedges to accommodate passersby. But he didn't like the idea. Feeling like a trespasser, he approached each new lawn cautiously to see if there were people having cocktails on their verandas.

Her mother, on the other hand, treated it as a great adventure. Each time her father complained that they'd come far enough, she would say, "Let's just see what's around this bend," and walk briskly out of sight. It was amusing to watch her parents relating so differently to private property. They were, after all, well-to-do themselves, though not so rich they could afford a mansion on a cliff.

Strolling along in the warm afternoon sun, she analyzed their behavior. He, of course, identified with the proprietors of these great homes. Her mother, however, was the poor little girl with her nose to the candy store window. Still not used to having money, she was fascinated by big houses as representing the magnificence of wealth.

The two danced their interesting ballet down the path, her mother rambling ahead, turning to look at everything like a rube in the big city, her father hanging back, then hastening forward and sending furtive glances right and left. She smiled uneasily as she watched them. It was unsettling to realize that she, sworn enemy of wealth and privilege, was just as entranced and intimidated before the houses of the rich as they were. Without realizing it, she had added her own step to the dance.

After about twenty minutes of walking, they ventured onto the lawn of an elderly woman who was having a cup of something on her porch. "Good afternoon," the woman called out gaily and waved her fingers at them. "Beautiful day for a walk, isn't it?" The three trespassers smiled gratefully and waved back. When they reached the walk's end, they were all agreeably tired and satisfied with themselves.

They took another memorable walk two days before leaving the island. John and Anne invited them to dinner and afterward suggested taking a night stroll through the town.

"You'll love walking in town at night," Anne said, donning a hand-crocheted shawl. "You can look in all the windows and see how people furnish their homes. No one ever pulls down a shade."

Out in the street a mild breeze caught at their clothing and touched their faces. The narrow cobbled lanes and ancient houses were bathed in the darkness and deep silence of a country town at night. There were no street lamps, but here and there a lighted window framed a warm domestic scene.

They walked slowly, listening to the sounds of their footsteps on the cobbles. She was flooded with a sense of peace and safety. Of all the occasions she had walked outdoors at night, this was the first in years which was not spoiled by a vague apprehension of danger.

"The tourists from the city are funny," Anne was saying to the others. "They never walk anywhere at night. They always drive and keep their car doors locked."

John laughed. "They have a terrible attitude. We're always glad when the season is over."

Her head filled suddenly with images. Walking along a busy street at mid-morning. Two men in a car circling the block and shouting obscene insinuations at her averted face. The feel of keys between the fingers of her clenched fist as she climbed uneasily up the dark stairway to her apartment. Waking abruptly to the sound of sirens whining through the night.

The family were talking about other things now, but she had no desire to join them. The pleasure of the night was gone and all she could think about was their smugness. The world was crawling with horror, but people with money and privilege could escape it. There were little islands of safety where these people went. Islands accessible to her, if she chose. Suburbs. A-frame houses in the country. Cabins in the mountains. Nantucket. Places so perfect and tranquil that the rest of the world seemed unreal.

One couldn't spend one's life taking nature walks and admiring the way people decorated their homes. She felt herself growing morose and sullen again, and wished she could suppress it but knew she could not.

They were laughing up ahead and touching each other's elbows to guide one another in the darkness. Her father, as usual, was a little in front scouting out hazardous obstacles. "Watch it—there's a curb here … Honey, be careful of that corner. If a car comes they won't be able to see you … " filling up his safe world with small dangers to control. But he felt them, she thought, as much as she felt hers, and was probably as full of anger over life's injustices as she. They dealt with their realities in different ways, and who knew which was right. Probably neither.

She would go back and subject herself to the suffocating smog of the city, the tedious part time job that allowed her time to write, her apartment in a neighborhood raw with robberies and rapes. And she would try to come to some conclusion about social obligations versus personal creativity. But she wouldn't find one, and would end by making compromises little different from those of her parents. So who was she to judge them?

A furious gale blew all night before the morning they were to go back to the mainland. Wind rattled the windows in great gusts, and rain was driven so hard that it seeped in under the panes and made puddles on the floors. It looked as if the ferry might be delayed for a day and she wasn't sure if this was disappointing news or not.

There was a great deal of work to do in shutting up the house, some of which would have to be undone if the ferry didn't run after all. All the treasures—the most irreplaceable and those with sentimental significance—had to be wrapped and packed away in the attic. Linens had to be washed and dried, lawn chairs brought in, trash taken to the dump. By noon the news was that the ferry was on its way and would leave for Woods Hole by 2:00.

They had an extra half hour in which to walk out to Smith Point for a sight of the storm-tossed ocean. Leaving her parents, she ran ahead like a child and scrambled up the grassy bluff which commanded a view of the beach. Down below, giant white breakers rolled in from far out at sea. Seagulls hovered over the water, their strong wings holding them steady against the buffeting wind and spray. Her heart was filled with a painful exhilaration. She longed to be free of the bonds of earth that limited her to standing and watching. She wanted to fly over the bluff and soar across the water, screaming hilarious gull screams, diving in after fish and emerging to bob up and down on the waves.

In few minutes her glasses were encrusted with salt. She took them off, but the view was slightly out of focus. Her parents were calling from below. It was time to leave.

They stood at the wharf for an hour in a fine drizzling rain. The boat bumped its awkward bulk between the pilings and unloaded its passengers, who emerged endlessly like clowns from a trick car. Loaded down with luggage, tennis rackets, and cameras, one after another they poised for a moment at the top of the gangway before trundling down the steps. A continuous stream of bicyclists pedaled out of the cargo hold ahead of the trucks and cars whose engines rumbled deep in the bowels of the boat.

These brave and cheerful tourists, jauntily waving to their friends and relatives on the wharf, had spent the two-hour ferry ride convincing themselves that the rain didn't matter. And now they would have a good time even though it might easily rain right up until they boarded the boat to go home again. She felt a poignant affection for them. She wished she could give them good weather and hoped their optimism would carry them through the holiday and send them back renewed.

When the last passenger was off, the crowd below gathered its bags, umbrellas and other trappings and nudged its way slowly up the gangplank like a throng of patient refugees. She pushed ahead to find seats together by a window. It was warm inside the cabin and the steamy glass was traced with rivulets of water. Wiping it clear with a sleeve, she gazed down into the waves that slapped against the boat.

Presently her parents joined her and then the great engine shuddered and churned the water and the boat began to move. They left their belongings and went outside to stand by the rail. It was still drizzling and windy but strangely mild. From inside, the air looked so much colder than it was that no one else had ventured out. She and her parents alone of all the passengers braved the elements to bid the island good-bye.

The wharf was already getting smaller, the town receding on its hillside, church spires disappearing in the mist. Rounding a curve of the harbor the boat pulled alongside the east jetty. She could just make out the cluster of boulders where she'd sat to write on those first few days. Soon the beach disappeared into the mist and they were in sight of the lighthouse.

"Got a penny?" her father asked her. "Throw a penny as you pass the lighthouse and it means you'll come back."

She watched them throw their pennies into the water. Then, struggling with the buttons on her coat, delving in first one pocket then another, she found her coin purse and pulled it out hurriedly, scattering coins about the deck. She dug in the purse until she clutched a penny between her wet fingers and threw it into the white water that churned behind the boat.

In a minute the lighthouse was gone, and so was the island, swallowed up in fog. The boat seemed to be moving more slowly now, as if feeling its way through the mist. Yellow buoys bobbed into view, floated alongside, and were left behind. A small cluster of seagulls hovered low above the rail. Startlingly close, they hung in mid-air like birds in a museum case. Their beaks opened to emit weird cries and their sharp black eyes stared brazenly.

It was very still on deck. The engine noises, the wind, the wash of waves against the boat, even the sharp gulls' cries were all muffled by the thick yellow air. Surrounded by this peculiar bland atmosphere and black water, the boat seemed to float in a timeless vacuum. They stood at the center of it for several minutes and then her parents moved to go back inside and she followed.

End of Summer

IT WAS AUGUST. The afternoon sun baked the pavements. I stepped from the car, pulled my damp shirt away from my back and fanned the skin abstractedly. Squinting against the glare, I inspected the shrubbery bordering the woods. There had once been a path there that connected our yard with the apartment houses behind. We kids had created the path ourselves with our numerous trips to the playground.

We used to climb the swing-set poles like monkeys after coconuts, and slide down the slide on waxed paper. The playground was supposed to have been reserved for the apartment dwellers only, but no one ever threw us out. We'd been coming there so long they must have thought we lived there too.

I pushed through the weeds and bushes where the path would have begun, and came almost immediately to the clearing where the treehouse had stood. No tree left. I wondered if it had died from being climbed so often.

Only fifteen or twenty yards away was the south edge of the old back yard. I was amazed to find the distance so much shorter than I remembered it. Once, our trip along that narrow path through waist-high grass and towering woods had been a safari. Now the jungle was gone, and I was a grown person, knee-deep in weeds.

The yard is going to be much, much smaller, I told myself, trying to prepare for the loss. I wondered if it would even be recognizable, with the house gone and an apartment building in its place.

For several minutes I stood there, reluctant to move on. The air was dusty and hot and smelled of dry mown grass. A bee buzzed in the distance.

. . .

Over twenty years before, my brothers and I had run barefoot over that great expanse of lawn. We'd climbed the twisted old fruit trees and swung by our knees from the branches. In winter, we had trampled huge pie-shaped paths through the snow and chased each other around them in games of fox and geese.

The back yards along our street were excessive. It was the primary reason our parents had bought the house. "For the children," they said. Having spent the first six years of their parenthood cooped up with us in a Chicago tenement, they were dazzled by all that space. So were we. The yard stretched out before us, green and endless. Beckoning: Come and play!

Nearest the house it was shady and cool. Iris and lilies of the valley, phlox and violets grew wild along the south edge. On the other side was a pebbly driveway and dilapidated garage covered over by morning glory vines. The garage was a popular structure to climb despite repeated admonitions by our father. He spent much of his time worrying about our drowning, getting in cars with strangers, slipping and falling from high places.

There were other perilous and fun things to climb in this part of the yard; among them a barbecue pit of unknown vintage, built of rocks and cement. It loomed mountainous over our heads. We loved to scramble up its side and shout echoes into the old rusted cylindrical chimney. This part of the yard also contained a rickety swing set which tilted dangerously off its base when anyone swung too high.

Sweet-smelling lilac bushes and a prolific walnut tree marked the beginning of the second part of the yard, a sunny, cheerful stretch of lawn dotted with the fruit trees—apple, crabapple, peach and pear.

This was where we played involved and complicated imaginary games. In an outsized, weathered sandbox we constructed intricate villages of sticks and grass and walnut shells. We built sand castles and filled the moats with water from the garden hose. We sometimes found little dried turds floating in these moats, since the sand box also served as a lavatory for neighborhood cats. No one minded particularly. Cat turds belonged in the sandbox as much as fermenting apples belonged under the apple tree.

Opposite the sand box was an ancient playhouse. The floor boards were soft to stand on and the heads of rusty nails protruded from the window casings where makeshift curtains had been hung and left to rot. Being so nondescript, the playhouse lent itself to the most diverse imaginary purposes. One day it was the cozy drawing room of an English manor house, complete with high tea laid out on hollyhock cups and saucers. The next day it was an abandoned miner's shack with three people trapped inside by the raging waters of a flash flood.

An elderly pear tree edged up against the playhouse as if for warmth or a friend to lean on in its old age. It was always a mystery why the tree blossomed every spring but never bore fruit. We were understandably ignorant about the genetics and geriatrics of plant life.

In summer when the lawn was mown, we raked the cut grass into large soft piles and fell on top of them. In the fall, we jumped in piles of leaves, immersing ourselves in the smell and feel of dry, crackling autumn. In winter we built elaborate forts populated by snow people. Regardless of the season, we seemed never to feel hot or cold or tired or bored, but played on and on.

. . .

The last bit of yard, beyond the fruit trees, was a large unshaded open space, half of which was planted each year as a vegetable garden. We had peas and beans, asparagus, lettuce and corn. Raspberries and strawberries grew along the borders, and wild mint, which we gathered for our parents' iced tea. We enjoyed the harvesting but protested the use of child labor in the weeding and watering of such a huge agricultural undertaking.

In August, we played hide and seek among the corn stalks which grew high over our heads. It amused us to watch the cats pick their way carefully through the rows, chew delicately on a blade of grass, and curl up in the shade of a wide-leafed rhubarb.

Our yard was made private by thick grape vines covering the fence along one side and the wooded lot on the other. The people who lived next door had a daughter my age named Renee, an only child who was not allowed to go anywhere or do anything. Only on rare occasions was she given permission to play in her yard, one equally as large as ours but manicured and landscaped to such perfection that, like a room in which you mustn't touch anything, it was not habitable by a child.

Renee would stand close to the fence and peer at us through the grape vine. We sometimes urged her to come over and play, but she always shook her head. Her excuse was that she preferred to play in her pool, the only object her parents gave her which might be called a toy. It was a plastic pool, much bigger than ours, and we envied her for it, unmindful of how much more entertaining it was to splash in a small pool with three than to wade in a large one alone. In winter she didn't come out at all.

• • •

I remained for a long while in the still heat of the woods among the weeds and buzzing insects. Just beyond sight of this idyllic yard of my childhood, I hesitated to step out of the thicket of weeds into the sunlight and find it forever gone.

The yard before me was a flat, narrow strip of grass, interrupted only by a small, lone tree. The grapevines had disappeared from along the fence. No flowers marked the southern edge. The playhouse, the sand box, the swings, the garage, all gone, making of the barren yard a uniform sun-burned plot, undistinguished by any detail.

The sky hung over me, relentlessly blue, and I wished for the company of a cheerful cloud to shade me from the glare. Walking slowly, as in a dream, I searched for some vestige of the past. But the yard was utterly empty.

In earlier decades, the grown-ups had reclined there on lawn-chairs late in the afternoon, sipping iced tea. But now there was no shade to recline beneath and no children turning somersaults to watch. It was a yard never visited. I felt over-sized and conspicuous, but I couldn't leave. I needed some tangible evidence that it really had been different once, some landmark that would put the bare tract into its right proportions.

Then, after careful searching, I found it, half buried in the weeds along the fence. It was a piece of gray and rotting board, all that was left of the old playhouse. It filled me with a sad fascination, and I knelt on the ground to touch the wood, a tombstone for a dead childhood.

But I was an inappropriate ghost to haunt the silent, sunbaked plot. I got up and walked quickly across the lawn and up the driveway, looking back only for a moment to see if a spindly barefoot little girl with a pale face might be waving good-bye.

That's Your House

ACROSS THE STREET, THE little girls are soaking their heads in the sprinkler. From the crabapple tree the cardinal insists on *Peter, Peter, Peter, Peter, Peter, Peter, Peter.* Who is Peter? The leaves of my Centaurea Montana droop in the direct sun, but the flowers are as blue as you could want. The little girls giggle. The younger one had to be coaxed by example several times before she could bring herself to jump into the heart of the spray. Now she's forgotten her fear of it.

Everything dances in the breeze except Flo's American flag at the end of the block. The flag stirs sadly. It's thinking of all the dead in all the glorious ignoble wars. Tomorrow is Memorial Day. Did Flo lose someone in a war? She divorced her husband in old age. Maybe she herself served in Korea? Or loved someone who did.

All the old people on the block with their histories. But no, there is only Flo left, and the Laws, with their righteous anger toward "these people who want a free ride." "These people" doesn't refer to run-away capitalists.

But Ken and Ruth Law work so hard picking up every fallen leaf and acorn by hand in their impeccable yard. And it can't be easy for Ruth with her bent spine and asthma, or Ken with his heart condition.

The new people strip their floors, an unmistakable droning of the sander coming through the open door of a newly empty house. Betty moved out this week after forty years on the block. A life-time battle with depression, lost, even before her husband died. He'd gotten a job at Walmart offering carts to customers just to get out of the house, and she was hurt by this. When neighbors sympathized, she cried. It will be pleasant to have in her place a young, happy, go-getter couple who sand floors. But still, Betty was a fixture in the neighborhood. The

Laws shook their heads. "She wouldn't ask for help!" Neither would they have, not with their philosophy of life.

This afternoon I poured buckets of aluminum phosphate solution into the roots of the hydrangeas to make the flowers come out blue. BLUE! It's not easy to grow flowers that will give you blue. I hate having to wait. Bloom *now*.

The motion of the porch swing redirects my recalcitrant brain chemistry which insists on urging me to fight or flee when there's no reason to do either. Generalized anxiety. Pounding heartbeats that shake the bed sometimes. But they are no match for a porch swing. The air sits on my shoulders like cashmere.

It's going to storm tonight. The clouds are drifting in. And here comes the big young woman, Karen Barnes, to sweep her sidewalk after mowing. She lives in the duplex to my right. Nose rings, earrings cascading down one ear, oversized white T-shirt that reveals every roll of flesh. She leads a life of friendships and neighborly responsibilities (though she is only a renter), and the occasional companionship of a borrowed dog. She is confident and competent and willing.

She and her pal Sam are going to fix my fence for the price of a six-pack of beer. Wouldn't take money. "We have fun doing projects together." Her father drives a truck cross-country. Her mother is starting to have some worrisome memory lapses. When Ken Law was taken off by ambulance with a mild heart attack in the middle of the night, Karen called her parents, sobbing.

The other new-ish neighbors walk their tiny dachshund morning, evening and night. Its name is Boris. I can't remember theirs. Cynthia, next to Flo, has two fat French bulldogs who look like her and are referred to as The Boys. Her breasts she calls The Girls, recounting a favorite story, how she lost a diamond earring, which turned up later, it having fallen into her bra and been rescued by one of Her Girls.

Cynthia wears a cross on a chain around her neck, but I heard her use the word "shit." You can never peg anyone. She has legs like huge linked sausages, but she mows her own lawn in shorts, works on her garden beds, and walks The Boys on even the hottest, most humid days. She has one of those solid constitutions that can withstand obesity. Hers is a social life revolving around food.

Cynthia and "The Sisters," Phyllis and Bev, who live in a cottage around the corner, came to my house the first time for dinner last night. They reappeared this morning to whisk me away for brunch at The Nook, their weekend hangout, and afterward invited me to a cookout at their house tonight at six. To my diffident explanation that I had to get some work done, they asserted, "But you'll have to eat something anyway!" Phyllis and Bev divorced their husbands, bought a house, and have lived together ever since, just as they did growing up.

Across the street, the little girls are still squealing in the sprinkler and now a grownup is on hand. Probably Sasha. Their front door is hidden by my rhododendron bush. Sasha and Deb adopted four children from as many countries and are fostering one child and have two dogs, a cat, and the occasional foster animal (last week it was a piglet). Sasha is the director of the city animal shelter, her life devoted to genial, no-nonsense care-giving. Five-year-old Elias has come outside. "Oh my god! What the hell are you doing!" I hear him shout. He is chastised. Has he picked up the language from day care or television? Sasha and Deb adopted him as an infant from Haiti. He greets and calls all the neighbors by name.

All last week Elias and four-year old China, the current foster child, unceasingly raced their training wheel bikes the length of the block and back before finally being able to exclaim to every passerby, "We can ride on two wheels now!"

The children play endless games on our dead-end street as if this were the 1950s. Deb's mother, Flo, in the bungalow at the end, has a block-long backyard that can only be described as a child's paradise. A daily parade of children pass my porch on their way to Grandma's house.

Now I find I'm starting to get hungry. I may take The Sisters up after all on their invitation to the cookout. Before I stop writing, though,

I must mention our neighborhood crazy person—Mary Ella—who works naked in her front yard on occasion and snatches up everyone's yard waste bags before the city can collect them. The bags sit in piles all around her house, along with other gardening refuse—plastic pots, etc. She's letting the yard waste rot until spring when she'll use it to mulch her entire property. She wants no grass or weeds.

Her incessantly barking dogs bring the police to her door periodically, called by various ones of us, and she is proud of having reduced their barking by chastising them according to the advice of the Dog Whisperer on the Discovery Channel. The change is barely noticeable, but at least there has been a change.

She says she loves "yard art." Looked at individually, any one item stacked on her porch and around her front yard might be considered attractive, or at least interesting. Taken all together, they make the yard a dump.

She has proudly declared herself to be a "compulsive hoarder." Last summer, she tied a serendipitously grown sunflower the height of a small tree to the guttering of her house with a rope fashioned out of plastic bags tied together. ("It cost me nothing!").

The city cited her for violating the property maintenance code. She promised to clean up things and loaded much of the junk into her pickup truck which she then parked a few blocks away. After the city came back to inspect and left, she drove the truck back and kept everything inside it, freeing up space to pile more stuff on her porch and lawn.

She has only one breast and never hides the lopsidedness of her Amazon chest. She is sixty-eight years old, exquisitely beautiful, and has no sense of boundaries between herself and others. "What's yours is mine" seems to be her philosophy. She moved in two years ago, replacing the tidy, industrious little family who lived there before. The Laws are appalled.

Within fifteen minutes of my meeting Mary Ella, she managed to tell me the details of her lawsuit against the car company from which she leases her car, her eviction from her condominium by the "snooty university types" who made up the condo association, the betrayal thirty-eight years ago of a lover who ran off with a teenager, and her several life-threatening illnesses including the cancer that took her breast.

Following that, she asked me to run some errands for her, though she has the pickup truck and a car parked in her driveway, blocking the sidewalk. There is no space for them in her two-car garage. She is my next door neighbor on the other side from Karen Barnes. I keep my distance.

Now it's just six o'clock. I'm definitely hungry. A little stiffly, I get up from the porch swing and start down my front walk toward The Sisters' house.

"HI!" shouts Elias, standing in the middle of his driveway. "That's YOUR house!" he says, pointing.

"You're right," I call back. "It is!"

The Roof Terrace

JUST THROUGH MY KITCHEN door is a roof terrace covered in gritty asbestos paper and sealed with tar. There is a rusty chimney pipe in the middle, protruding from who knows what inner recesses of the house. When it rains, a pond accumulates in a large depression surrounding the chimney pipe, giving the effect (slight) of a submarine just below the surface.

I sit on the terrace in a chair which I retrieved from a trash heap once, a wooden lawn chair painted grass green and covered with green, orange and red striped canvas. It's a bit rump-sprung, which is what makes it comfortable, like a broken-in shoe.

A tree growing next to the roof has long brown pods hanging from it and I think there is something narcotic in those pods because the cats rub up against them with ecstatic expressions on their faces and then roll around on the roof with their bellies bared to the world.

If I had some good strong binoculars, I could spy on about four or five hundred people from my roof terrace, living as I do in what the urban renewal people would call a congested neighborhood. In fact, the houses are so close together that sometimes, standing at the edge of my roof, I am tempted to see if I could, with a good running start, leap to the roof next door. It could be done—not by me, maybe—but by someone.

There is a lovely (though if you think about it, ominous) haze that suffuses the view from my roof. The haze sits gently on a tier of old brick apartment buildings perched along the hill that constitutes my farthest horizon. The apartments have rows and rows of windows which face east and glow hot and orange in the morning as if fires raged behind them.

At no time, day or night, can you sit on my roof terrace and not have your ears filled with a low, whispery roar. Between the hours of seven to nine a.m. and four to six p.m. during the week, the roar is a true roar, not whispery at all. But at four in the morning on a Sunday, it's more like a long, drawn-out sigh. At all times this ambiguous sound is punctuated by sharper ones. Little screams pierce the air during the day and can usually be pinned down to cats, children or birds. A loud bold laugh and the metallic tinkling of a beer can rolling along a gutter frequently interrupt the night.

From a roof terrace in the city it's easy to feel omnipotent, but my roof terrace has a way of bringing me down to earth with an unwelcome reminder of my mortality. It sports a rickety and weather-beaten fire escape railing which, if you venture close enough to the edge of the terrace to experience that universal sensation of being inches from annihilation, you will find is attached to a fire escape stairway. Thus I am frequently reminded that someday (for instance, the day the second floor tenant goes to work leaving his gas ring lit with a pan of bacon grease sitting in it) the windows in my apartment house could glow hot and orange and it wouldn't be the reflection of a sunrise.

That's one unsettling reminder of my mortality. The other is that the fire escape stairway communicates directly with the ground, providing depraved persons with free and unhindered access to my home. I don't like to dwell on this, however, and usually don't.

My cats, Jane and Wanda, spend a lot of time on the roof and not infrequently I keep them company. On lonely, boring afternoons, when I'm suffering from ennui, they try their best to entertain me by running the length of the terrace and hurling themselves off the edge, *almost*. Then they sit down abruptly and lick imaginary filth from their paws. Their favorite part of this entertainment is when I lurch forward in my chair with a cry of horror on my lips. Afterwards, they look up from their toilette and fix me with an ironic gaze.

In winter, they leave crisscrossing trails of paw prints in the snow. The best trails are those that begin just beneath the kitchen door and end at the very edge of the roof with no tracks returning. The cats like to give the impression of having committed suicide. The way they manage it is to jump from the roof to a branch of the tree and then dig their claws in and shinny three stories to the ground.

The roof terrace is pretty cold in winter, exposed as it is to winds from three directions, and I usually don't venture out on it at that time of year but prefer to look at it through the steamy panes of my kitchen doors. When the terrace is covered with snow, it looks quite arctic and the chimney pipe gives the effect of there being a heated igloo underneath.

In summer, when the leaves are out, the terrace is not entirely un-protected from the sun. I spend the day shifting my chair across the roof a few inches at a time in order to stay within the moving patch of shade. Not that that's all I do. Between shiftings, I am writing short stories, memorizing lines for roles in plays, and talking to myself in various dialects. The roof terrace is my Muse. It shelters me and stimulates me and makes me feel smug about my existence. It's a fine place to be if you're in a creative mood or a pensive mood or a playful or romantic mood. A multipurpose venue, I call it.

I plan to have a party on it next week. I will string up little Japanese lanterns with candles in them and invite my guests to lounge about on deck chairs. The soft flickering lights will illuminate our faces in the darkness and voices will be carried through the summer night, mingling with the whispery roar of the city.

Tikal

LET ME TRY TO REMEMBER the impressions of this jungle, the first time of being in a jungle, knowing I was going to see these things I was about to see, the buildings that appeared silently in a clearing at the end of a bend in the path.

Here was the first building, immense but, as it turned out, one of the smallest I would visit. It sat squarely in this big cleared space with the sun beating down warmly and happily, parrots screaming in the sky. I had never seen parrots in the wild. Imagine! I thought, here I am, not knowing what to stare at most, the ancient structure or the ancient warming sky or these parrots flying in pairs like military fighters but not at all like military fighters because even though they flew like jets, streaking and arrow-like, they were free and they screamed and landed on treetops higher than any trees I'd ever seen.

I stood and stood, just rooted to the spot, a little way into the clearing, my eyes bulging some, frustrated at not being able to absorb these sights into a nerve center in my brain that could translate them into sensations—tastes, smells, touches, and emotions.

There were two buildings, one a shell, a ravaged duplicate of the other, its mirror image facing it, saying this is what it once looked like, like me. I ran forward and climbed up the stairs to the first level. The stones were real. I had my hands on them. They had been there for maybe three thousand years and they were still here in this dense jungle, not just here but intact, climbable.

I scrambled to the top, out of breath, and looked down on everything. There were carved stones—altar stones, supposedly—at regular intervals between the two structures. From the top their significance seemed much greater. These had had a function. The carvings had talked just as much as my map did or the numbers and dials on my watch. People had known what those stones were for, could read them and act accordingly.

The silence was so eerie and so sad. Nostalgia, loneliness, elation fluttered about my eyes, trying to fill them with tears. The place was alive with ghosts. Screaming in unison, the parrots shot off again, leaving a trail of echoes.

Below, a young man in khaki shorts and garlanded with cameras, stepped out into the clearing. It was beautiful to see him. He looked up at me, and I down at him, without shyness and I smiled, shook my head slowly, held out my arms and called, "Are we really here?"

He took my picture. I watched him wander among the stones and ruined walls, putting them into perspective—they were built to accommodate crowds and he was dwarfed. He disappeared. I couldn't hear his footsteps because the jungle was so dense and so damp it swallowed the subtler sounds. Maybe this was why parrots screamed. I had read there were howler monkeys in the trees too.

How could these buildings ever have been built? I didn't like to think people could have been so determined, so dogged as to have engaged in this harrowing labor when it would seem to have been unnecessary. Couldn't people have been content to live in a house on poles with a thatched roof? To worship stalks and ears of corn, the moon and the sun, simply accepting the abundance of these things and be satisfied? Why did they go to such dramatic extremes?

They didn't have metal tools or even pack animals. Why did they do this to each other? Someone had to carve these stones, hacking them out of hillsides and hauling them miles through jungle. It was horrible to imagine the hardship. It felt like being somewhere where a crime has been committed. I had a lump in my throat.

The young man's head and then his shoulders appeared at the edge of the platform where I was standing. He hopped nimbly up and stood quietly gazing out at the scene. It was such a relief to be near another human being. I liked the quiet way he took pictures and was alone like me.

Having this little contact gave me the courage to continue along the path through the jungle, knowing I wasn't completely alone and that it was all right to experience these things by myself. Other people did it. He had cameras, but then I had eyes.

Slowly I climbed back down, crossed the clearing and found the path indicated by a small sign that said "Great Plaza," with an arrow pointing into the jungle.

Now the path snaked up and down some small ridges, following or accompanied by what I suddenly realized were paving stones. This was an old road. Every few yards, there they'd be, thick stones some scattered about, some as if laid yesterday, flat and tidy, edge to edge, a road where people had walked with piles of laundry or pots of water on their heads. People chatting and urging children to catch up. A street, in fact, like Main Street or Madison Avenue.

I heard the monkeys for the first time then, not howling, but crashing through the canopy. Leaves and twigs fell at my feet and I looked up. There they were, high above, hanging by an arm or a tail for a moment, then flinging themselves with great speed from branch to branch, chasing each other up and down, camouflaged in the foliage as soon as they stopped moving. I had to support my head with one hand to keep looking up. It made me dizzy, they were so high and so elusive. I quit seeking them and moved on.

I began to feel expectant. It was like when I had been driven to the ocean as a child. As fields gave way to marshes, and marshes to dunes, to unbroken sky, no trees, no buildings or telephone poles because over the next rise would be this enormous gleaming thundering ocean or if not over that rise, then over the next one or the rise after that, but soon. You could smell it, feel it on your skin, hear the accompanying sounds—gulls, wind. And you would be excited, anxious, impatient.

This is how it was as I walked along the path. I could feel something monumental up ahead. I had not been prepared by the clearing I had just left. I had been given a taste of what was to come, enough to think it might be more intimidating and just as sudden as the ocean. I braced myself by walking more slowly. And the next rise brought a change in terrain, a large hillock with stones toppled along its sides, the jungle pushed back and a wide path of packed dirt leading around to the back of the hill. It was going somewhere.

I heard the sounds of distant little voices, not damped by jungle but bouncing lightly off large hard surfaces. The path was packed hard and slippery. I climbed on hands and knees. Coming to the top, I rounded the side of the hill.

Temple of the Great Jaguar. Temple of the Masks.

Oh, these stubborn people, what had they done? Lost all sense of proportion, deluding themselves that they were giants.

Acknowledgements

MY HEARTFELT THANKS AND APPRECIATION TO:

Caryl Lyons for her careful and astute reading of the manuscript.

Lucy Luxenburg for listening to me perform the stories as they unfolded.

Niki Harris (for pointing out where pseudonyms were needed. "I just want to protect you from libel suits." Indeed!).

YouTube for distracting me from the state of our government by broadcasting kittens sleeping atop golden retrievers.

Google for answering the most trifling and incoherent questions and for conjuring up perfect/exact/precise/dead-on/ideal/masterly/apt synonyms at the click of the mouse.

KATE KASTEN lives and writes in Iowa City, Iowa. In an earlier phase of her life, she wrote, performed and toured a solo act—Kate Kasten Comedy-Theatre. A number of her monologues appear in this book. After a decade of portraying eccentric characters on stage, Kasten switched to fiction and is the author of five novels, a book of fairy tales for adults, two short story collections, two memoirs and a book of poetry. Her short fiction has appeared in *Glimmer Train, American Literary Review, Madison Review,* and *Northwest Review.* Recently she has turned to parody and political satire, with *Alice's Adventures in Trumpsterland & Alice in the House of Glass, Cautionary Tales,* and *Banners,* which takes on the subject of book-banning.